THE WANDERING WORLD:

AND OTHER STORIES

B C WOODRUFF

IAN MORGENHEIM

For permission requests, write to the publisher, addressed to the address below.

Shatter Books
www.ShatterBooks.com

To contact Shatter Books: shatterbooks@gmail.com.
Illustrations By: Karston Smith
Cover design by Rebecacovers

ISBN-10: 0995170207
ISBN-13: 978-0995170209

For You.

The Tower

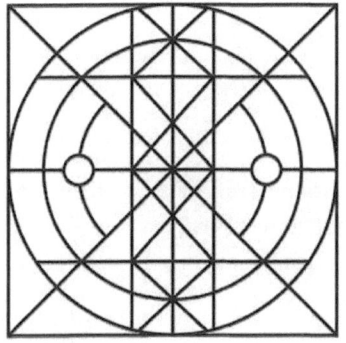

REVISION
TWELVE

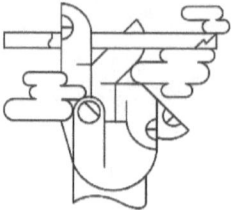

"George Orwell was pretty close when he wrote perhaps his most recognized piece of work, Nineteen Eighty-Four, back in 1948. He just didn't know it. We call this type of cultural or social contamination a 'runoff' or a bleed and it's fairly well-documented, though there's no easy explanation for why it happens or why it only happens to certain people."

"We can trace the modern day Revisionists back to the time before the library of Alexandria burned. People back then had it a lot easier, let me tell you. They didn't have to contend with modern technology and a global society where information travels from one side of the planet to a thousand places across with a single click. But that's all part of the job, I suppose."

Martin cleared his throat and went on:

"As I was saying. George Orwell had it pretty close. "When I'm tasked with explaining to newcomers what it is we do, and specifically what it is we did to them to prepare the way, I always present them with the same 'comfort package' consisting of the following items:

"One – A copy of Nineteen Eighty-Four with freshly-bound commentary written by my predecessor. He loved the classics. He hated Harry Potter, though that really just sets him apart from most people these days. A true contrarian that one, always obsessed with taking notes and documenting the world. It's such a shame – as per protocol, everything I gave him but that flimsy and faded book was thoroughly Edited.

"You're wondering what I mean when I use that word in this context, I'm sure, but that will come later.

"I offer my recruits a copy of that dystopian classic to remind them that no matter how clear the clues might be, in fiction or fact, the untrained mind is apt to ignore them. We are Forgotten by design.

"The book does contain its fair share of rambling – if not wholly incoherent – notes in the margins, but they are simply meant to marinate the ego before we scour it clean with the flames of insight. "Hmmm. Perhaps that was a poor choice of words, given the situation.

"For the sake of brevity, allow me to tell you what you already know, Detective. You've discovered that no matter how far you reach out or what level of government you connect with that the bodies that have led us here, well, they simply... do not exist.

"These people have never had a bank account. They have never had a relation. Never had kids. Never went to the park on Sun- days. Never ate a lunch or paid a bill. One, who I knew quite well, was never born to parents and rewarded with the gift of life and the name Raymond Winters. His sister never had a younger brother who she once kicked off a swing set in their backyard at age four. This event didn't result in a hairline fracture to his wrist that went unnoticed. And that, in turn, certainly didn't cause him so much pain in the years that followed.

"According to all extant documentation and most loving memory, this man never existed. Anyone who would have remembered him is gone, except for a few of us in the Ministry.

"That's right. Good ol' Eric Arthur Blair came pretty close – even got the wording right on that part and more than a few others.

"Two – I give them a bundle of paper with five coloured pens to write out their questions. Now, we don't call it Newspeak and I won't bore you with the grammatical particulars. It doesn't really matter. What you'll like to know is that it's a very colourful script. It involves using specific hues to help emphasize certain concepts that conventional orthography can't. Replacing adjectives, notably, and illuminating the emotional spectrum through the visual. "It was developed simply because of a question one of our esteemed leaders posed: 'Are we blind to colour? No? Well, why do we write as though we are?'

"I ask them to keep the questions simple so that I can answer them simply. I don't like complicating matters. "Why" is a simple question, perhaps the simplest there is, and even that takes skill and precision to answer.

"Three – I give them a ticket up to a cottage in Vermont. They're expected to spend a week there by themselves without the bother of outside distractions. We always send them in late fall just as the first snowfall is fast approaching. This, and number four, are pretty much standard. Unlike many of my counterparts, however, I provide detailed directions to ensure they aren't lost along the long stretches of dirt road that you have to follow to find the spot.

"Four - I give them a backpack with some simple supplies like food and candles. I wrap a bottle of alcohol, usually whiskey, in a slim blanket to fight off the cold and a note that asks them to drink it only if they need to.

"Everyone pretty much finds the need to. "It's a lot to take in. "With these supplies in hand we ship them up to their – well, initiation isn't altogether the right word. It's also not entirely the wrong one. Then we pick them up at the end of the week. Most people recover in some form or another. They have questions, but most are ready to hear what we have to say. Some are still in a state of shock and we baby them a bit. And once – well, once that I'm aware of – we found a man hanging in the second floor stairwell.

"We don't leave rope there anymore. "I had a good feeling about the last one I sent, but, as you can imagine... I guess that feeling was a little misplaced, right?"

Martin paused. He'd done just about everything he could to expose the secrets he was taught to guard till his death. That people could be erased, made to toil in shadow for the greater good. Well, as far as he could see it, death wasn't too far away and it wouldn't make much difference if one person knew the truth at the end of the day. If they were even prepared to accept it as such.

"I'm more than a little confused." Across from Martin Schwartz sat Detective Benjamin Anabath. He adjusted his posture and stretched his back against the worn leather of the interrogation room seat.

Benjamin squinted at the man and crossed his arms, determined to understand but finding himself lost in a tangled web of questions that struggled – and failed – to coalesce properly. The detective's left hand came up, stroked his strong jawline, and fell back into place. There was a scar there only partially covered by a five o'clock shadow that seemed to thicken even as they sat in the cold interrogation room in Charlotte, Vermont.

Martin knew the look. It wasn't only confusion. It was a growing anger borne from ignorance. Itself, begot from a desire to believe and a refusal to do so.

"Where did I lose you?" Martin asked, crossing his legs. "Pretty much at the beginning. I've never read this 'Eric Arthur Blair' you mentioned."

"Hmm, I suppose that makes sense." Martin smiled and nodded. "I guess I could go into greater detail if you like. I know it pretty much by heart."

Benjamin shook his head. "No. I don't care about your little club, I just want to know what happened on the night of the twelfth." He tapped his pen against a fresh sheet of paper that was embossed with the impatient scrawls of a heavy-handed colleague. Even from his position, Martin could see a few faint words attempting to make themselves known. Words like murderer and alibi.

"Can you be specific?" Martin asked, trying to find anything the two of them had in common. "As you've seen, quite a lot has happened."

"I want to know why you were found walking out of an inferno that could have burned down the east side of Milford. I want to know why there was a body buried out back. I want to know why you seem so fucking relaxed about the whole ordeal. I want to know, if you'd kindly admit to it, why you did it. If you don't feel like sharing, well... I always find a way."

"I did mention Alexandria, didn't I?" Martin smiled helpfully. This only inflamed the anger of the middle-aged man with dark black eyes and thick, short hair.

"Who was she?"

"Really? Hmm. Not much of a history buff, are you?"

"Wouldn't peg myself as one, no. I'm more of what happened on the twelfth sort of guy. You follow me?"

"What about that movie back in, what was it, 2004? I think Oliver Stone directed that one. Bloody terrible and all that, but all the same. Wait." He put a bandaged hand to his head and concentrated. "Hold on. Almost got it. Ah! Yes. Colin Farrell – he was our King of Macedonia in that version." He smiled and looked up. "Terrible movie, but..."

The detective's look had not changed. "Let me guess – you're not much of a movie guy, either?"

10

"The twelfth."

"Right. The twelfth. Well, as I was saying, sometimes we have a bit of a hard time when people are first brought into our... you called it a club and I have no problem with that... and this new fellow, Thomas Bridgeman, fit into that category with qualifications to spare. I got a call from him just three days after he'd arrived at our 'resort getaway' in Charlotte. He was frantic. Said that someone was after him. Said that when he arrived at the house, he felt as if someone was watching him. All very dramatic, this guy. It's why I liked him. He had a way with words. Poor man claimed that his first night at the cabin, he spotted someone wandering outside his bedroom. Only, when he went out to look there weren't even snow prints. Now, I took him as being a little bit put off because of the reading material I'd given him, but as it turned out, he never got around to opening it. Lazy brat he turned out to be." Benjamin scribbled and whispered, "Yes, Thomas Bridgeman. Go on."

"So, I told him I'd go up and make sure everything was alright. Entirely against protocol, I hope you understand, but I had a feeling that there was something odd about the whole situation. Suffice it to say that the drive up was tense."

"And you found the body some time after you arrived?"

"Correct."

"And you brought it back to Milford. Tampering with a crime scene."

"Yes. It was not standard procedure, but I had my reasons." Benjamin's eyes widened – finally, something approaching a confession. "Let's say for just a moment that you're telling the truth, and that bringing Bridgeman back is all you did. Do you have anyone who can collaborate your story? Someone you were with at the time of the murder? We found no records of any- one matching his description. No one has claimed him missing. But we asked around the neighbourhood, and turned up an old rental agreement..." He looked over the paper. "Thomas S. Bridge- man. Lists his address as Apartment 102 in Valleyfield Tower on Rikards Street. But when we investigated, we found that no one had lived there for months. Where was he from, really?"

Martin's eyebrow went up. "Benjamin, all except two of the people I've known for the best years of my life were swallowed up by the fire you've just accused me of causing." He paused. "So no, I don't have anyone that will, and I think the word you wanted was corroborate, my story. I'll also add that Thomas Bridgeman was born in a small town in northern Vermont. Actually in a small community in a maple orchard near the border. I doubt that will help you any, though." He sighed. "Do you mind if I smoke?"

"Go ahead." The detective shrugged and Martin pulled out a Violent Belle branded cigarette from his pocket.

"Bad habit, I know, but it helps with the stress." Martin's hands came up and Benjamin noted how they were shaking now under the bandages. He was nervous. This was what he was hoping for.

He looked at the red spots dotting the white. The bastard had deserved it, hadn't he? He'd been burned rather badly there, and on his back.

"All of this happened on the tenth, correct? Leading

up to the fire that started late at night on the eleventh?"

"Yes, sir."

"What happened between the tenth and the twelfth, Martin? And what did you need that body for?" The detective avoided the smoke being blown in his direction.

"Well, we checked over his timeline and did what we do with anyone who leaves our organization – whether by choice or by... incident. We performed a brief forensic analysis, interred the body on the estate, edited his life, and moved on."

"Edited?"
"I'd normally refer back to the book, but your severe lack of cultural knowledge is making these explanations take a lot longer than I would like them to. I will make do with the time I have." He cleared his throat. "My people are the reason you've only found a single document that suggests Bridgeman ever existed. Our numbers may be few, but our connections run deep. Databases, city archives – nothing is beyond us."

Delusions of grandeur? Benjamin wondered. "I see."

"I returned back to the campus – the manor at 243 River Rock Drive – and went back to work on finding new candidates. We used to get forty or fifty a year when I was a boy, but people have other interests these days. YouTube and the Internet and designer drugs. Maybe it's our name. Maybe we're too good at our jobs. I don't know." He sighed. "The volunteers we do attract aren't always... shall we say worthwhile. Thomas had been a good find, and we were just as interested as anyone else in discovering who had committed that heinous crime. Yet it had appeared, by all accounts, to be an isolated incident. A stranger in the forest. We were blind to the possibility that the entire organization – not just a single facility – had been compromised. That Bridgeman's death was a warning shot."

"Are you saying this was premeditated murder then, Martin?"

"All of them, yes. Bridgeman and the rest."

"Just making a note." Benjamin wrote it down with a sarcastic question mark.

"Do as you like, it won't really make a difference. The people who were on the other side of this are far and gone by now."

"You'll leave that for us to decide, alright?" He was trying to sound sincere. He didn't. Martin folded his arms. "As you like." The smoke rolled over his shoulder. "I'm just trying to save you time."

"Go on."
"When they breached the perimeter of the campus, we were completely unprepared. The shadows had not failed us in decades, and we had grown complacent. The third watch, all seven of them, died without tripping an alarm. And these were professionals, detective, a far cry from initiates like Bridgeman. By the dawn we'd lost the entire campus and only

three of us were still breathing. If we managed to kill any of the attackers, I imagine you'll find that whatever 'evidence' there might have been has probably already vanished. If you found any to begin with." He yawned. "I bet they got the information on where to find us from poor Thomas before they killed him." He teared up a bit but maintained his strength.

"Such interesting stories you weave. You almost sound convincing." He leaned in. "Is that your story, then? You were attacked and you made it out of... 243 River Rock Drive just because you were lucky?"

"Not lucky. They let me go. They let the three of us go. It was meant to be five. At least that was how it was done in the old days. I don't think any of us truly believed their Order was still active." Martin finished his cigarette. "I collapsed into the fresh snow and was picked up by some paramedic. I woke up here. Alone. I'm assuming."

"Yes. Very suspicious, these situations of yours, Martin."

"I imagine you had a tip-off that I was the one who caused the fire?"

"Could be. I'm not at liberty to say." Detective Anabath smiled; the man was getting red in the face, and he was getting close to the answer he wanted. He just needed to apply a little more pressure. "Are you about ready to start telling the truth now? Let's go back and start with the basics, shall we?"

"If that's what you want. Not much time left now. Should have asked earlier."

"Sure, sure." He moved the pencil away as if it were a fly buzzing around his head. "You gave the name Martin Schwartz when you woke up."

"I did." Martin said. "Well, our records show no one by that name living at the place that burned down on 243 River Rock Drive. We've accounted for fifty-three of the fifty-three we picked up. Nothing about you, Mr. Schwartz. Care to elaborate? Or are you going to pretend that these people went back and"– he looked at his notes –"Edited you too?"

Martin's eyes went wide. "53 lies, detective. We are Forgotten; you shouldn't have found anything. Dig deeper. So many Edits at once... the Order must have–" Martin coughed, and his face flushed a deep red. No, not red. Purple. Benjamin was quick to catch on to what he was seeing. The man was choking. Choking on whatever had been in the cigarette. He reflected as he vaulted over the table that it had smelled a little odd. He'd assumed it was a menthol or some other flavoured brand. The man wheezed as Benjamin's fists came down and pounded on the door to the interrogation room.

"He's gone and poisoned himself! Get me Doctor Emerson!" It was too late. Martin was on the floor, foaming at the mouth. He would not let them win. Although, for those looking on, it was hard to see that he was smiling while the blood and bile oozed from his mouth. He was prepared for this, as the others were prepared to carry on without him.

The painful world receded. His mind held onto its

last thought. The others had made it. The work of the Forgotten – of the Revisionists – would continue, and true knowledge would be preserved against the ravages of human nature and time. The truth would persist and they would rebuild again.

There would be another Alexandria.

JELLY BEANS

"Heather?" the GenCell nurse asked quietly. She did not respond. "Miss Lambert?" The nurse knelt, adjusting her traditional red and blue habit. They were the colours of the GenCell Corporation. Her hair, neatly tucked below a deep crimson bonnet, and a face with only the slightest hint of coverup gave her an old-fashioned aura of propriety that inspired reverence and respect.

They weren't nuns, though. The GenCell Nurse's Manual told them to respond to nun or even sister if someone addressed them as such. For better or worse, it was an echo of a simpler time. GenCell called it Neo-Orthodoxy, a carefully-triangulated rebranding that struck a chord with those overwhelmed by a changing world. Unlike much of the competition, GenCell had already begun to change the conversation, transforming their corporate image to reach a growing global market.

The resurgence of religion after the events of L-Day inspired some inventive marketing ploys on GenCell's part. They unironically called their ever-expanding array of medical and social services Good Works, which provoked surprisingly little backlash from traditionalists. At the end of the day, as stock markets closed and consumer reactions were analyzed, the evidence was clear – the imagery they appropriated seemed to be helping their cause and extending their reach.

Heather was quiet, but had clearly heard the woman's question. "It's okay to be nervous," the nurse said. "A lot of people get nervous before the procedure." She sat down on the chair next to her and wrapped her gloved hands around Heather's pale flesh. They were still now, and this stillness extended into the silent choir of the waiting room.

"I... I don't know if I want this," Heather blurted out. "It's okay, honey. It's covered. The suit will keep you healthy until better treatments are developed." Heather didn't like that the woman was touching her. She'd always hated being touched. She had traced it back to a memory when she was younger. One that haunted her like a rustling in the walls of her mind. Like a rat chewing away at her innards. Like the disease she now carried. "Alright," Heather said after a moment. "Let's go." She stepped up and the nurse helped her along the long hall leading to the hermetically-sealed, aggressively sanitary room she had seen in all the tutorial videos after orientation.

"You'll see. Most people actually enjoy being encapsulated." The nurse smiled. "My brother had it done last year. He's never been better and he gets to watch his kids grow up. Do you have any–"

"No," Heather said abruptly. "Sorry. Yes. Of course not." The nurse went a little flushed. "I'm... sorry."

"It's fine. I don't think I would have made a very

good mother." Heather almost shrugged but the pain kept her from following through. She was beginning to hunch over, a sure sign that the painkillers were wearing off.

She thought about that: Painkillers? But they don't really kill the pain, do they? They just make it go away for a while. You can't say you're killing something when it just comes back. At best, it's a pain wall. Like a flimsy storm barrier holding back a torrent of neuron-flaring agony from drowning you. In the end the pain always comes back, though, doesn't it? Unless you do something to stop it altogether.

She didn't like thinking about that ultimatum. "We're here." The nurse pressed the small green button and eased Heather into the airlock between the anteroom and the operating theater.

Between two worlds, Heather thought, imagining what awaited her on the other side. She lingered in that thought, unaware at first that she had sent herself spiralling through her memories on a journey that would cut through the pain. Physically, she was unchanged, eyes staring ahead like blank canvases.

Suddenly, the ache and agony slid off her because her mind had taken her far enough away that it could focus on the time before.

She was here, but had bridged the mind to then. She was alive with optimism. Her adolescent years were filled with the expectations that the future would be... wonderful. It was a simpler time when GenCell was a name that only came up in conversation amongst the most diehard science

enthusiasts. But all the while, it was lurking and positioning –
and insinuating – itself into everything.

It was a shadow at noon. Hidden. Waiting. Barely
anyone had heard of them except in a general sense in those
days. Now... Well, now you could find a GenCell branch in
every major city across the planet. They even had facilities on
those lavish floating habitats – no surprise, given that they'd
financed them in the first place. They still owned most of
them, didn't they?

In fact, hadn't she read that the habitats' annual GNP
had superseded both the United States and China last year? It
was possible. Her trailing memory brought her back to an age
of wonder and curiosity.

Sixteen years old. A bright future ahead. Friends at
the park watching the boats pass through the locks separating
the Great North American Canal from the Atlantic Ocean.
They liked to sit there and drink stolen alcohol and pretend
they were on one of the ships heading out to sea. There was
one in particular she recalled in vivid detail. Wasn't it called
The Parrot? She thought so.

Her friends, Timothy Wilson and his sister Cherish,
were laughing when Heather breached the barrier between her
present self and this much younger, healthier version.

It was like escaping into a dream. Swallowed by a
chain of memories, she had a lifetime of possibilities to
explore, and like any author of presence and power she was
free to be her own god – to sift through important points
without losing a moment in the present.

If only her future self were able to command the past again, to pierce the temporal shell. She could have been warned about what fate had in store with her.

Such are the illusions of memory; and like ghosts, we are doomed to smile or scream at the decisions we made in passion and patience, long before the weight of years settled on our shoulders.

Heather observed her younger self shake free of reverie, pulling away from the size of the ships ahead of her and the green trees that stood between.

"Where's that one heading, Heather?" Timothy asked. "Probably out to Australia. I bet they have a bunch of seeds for their plantations in New South Wales. There's a man on board; he's wondering what the hell's the point of it all! Hmm. He definitely left his wife back in Chicago. She's cheating on him. It's all going downhill." She reached for the bottle of sticky, sweet ice wine and gave it a good pull. "He's thinking about killing himself but they're expecting a baby, and even though he knows she's unfaithful, there's a small chance that the kid is his. He wants to wait to find out. This trip is good for him, though. His bunk- mate is a Frenchman from Québec. He's brought a lot of booze and some cheese. Now, our guy's lactose intolerant but he's willing to risk it. You know, to keep life interesting?"

The two looked at her, entranced. They loved hearing Heather talk about almost anything. She had a penchant for grabbing the attention of those around her. It was a talent that evolved into a short career as a novelist prior to the invention of Seemore.

These days her work revolved around correcting computerized mistranslations and minor syntax errors.

They don't need writers anymore. Not real writers, at least. Someone went ahead and made them obsolete.

The programs turned out stories, and good ones at that, which were well-liked almost entirely due to their simple, formulaic grasp of convention. It's what the people wanted, and it just so happened that all we had to do was derive a clever algorithm or two to achieve what no government had ever accomplished: to take the written word away from the human mind.

Heather, like other writers, was relegated to working behind the scenes. Editing or adjusting elements here and there for flow and consistency. Creativity at the cost of creativity, but at the end of the day she didn't mind. It was still writing, even if it could only really be called that in a stretched and sort-of way.

Eventually, even Seemore was optimized to the point that her job was rendered redundant – and her employers found themselves struggling to keep out of the red. The closure of their central content office followed, and many of her people found themselves living in government-provided shelters, unable to make ends meet.

She had been one of the fortunate ones. Her friends at the parent company had eyes on her well before they trimmed the fat. Welcomed with open arms, she found herself standing on the brink of new opportunities, and accepted a managerial position for a new division they were going to open in China.

She could never say that the company treated her poorly.

All of this led to the reason she found herself here today. When she discovered the cancer it was too far along for conventional treatment.

There was another way, though... Heather eased herself into the present but focused on Timothy and Cherish, placing a finger slowly upon and then pushing down the airlock button. With a swirl of sterilized air passing her by, she stepped forward.

She focused on her resurfaced adolescent memories again.

Cherish smiled. "And? What happens next?"

"Well, he eats the cheese and has some real nasty diarrhea that gets him out of deck work. This is probably on purpose, but people believe him that it was a mistake. They make it out to sea and somewhere around New Caledonia they're boarded at night by a very organized group of pirates."

"Pirates!" Timothy yelped. "I love those guys."

"Not those kind of pirates, well, not really. These guys are New Caledonian separatists. They want to hold the cargo and the crew as ransom to fuel their war against the government."

"What do they want from the government?" a man, who had been sitting not far from them asked. Next to him sat...her.

"Uh..." Heather wasn't sure what to do. He nodded. "I didn't mean to upset your process. It's quite an imagination you got there, little lady." The man put his hand on her. "Truth is, back in the day my Margot used to be a writer. She had the same spark and talent to just–bam–make things interesting."

"Excuse me... sir?" Timothy asked, trying to make the three of them seem more innocent than bellowing around a bottle would suggest. The older man saw through the ruse and, in a condescending tone that made them feel terribly out of place, answered.

"Yes, boy?"

"Can... can she talk?" Timothy went a little pale. "Tim!" Cherish slapped him. "Don't be rude!" Words flashed across the strip of moulded plastigel that covered her mouth.

"i can speak. i can listen. your story is fun, little girl. please, would you finish it for us?" Under the mask she was smiling, her teeth shaded wine-red by the suspension fluid. To others, she looked something like a woman who had been placed in a flexible, plastic fish tank form-fitted to move along with her. A few inches of liquid and a plastic coat, transparent except as needed to preserve modesty. Like leftovers wrapped in clingfilm. At her hip, a small box with a tube leading into the side of her suit whirred and hummed. If Heather looked carefully, which she could hardly help, she could see the liquid inside was circulating somehow, maybe taking in oxygen.

"I... guess," Heather said, and went on. "So, the pirates board their ship, right? Well, our friend the Frenchman, he's not really a Québecer is he? No, he's part of the New Caledonian separatists! Been that way all along. As the rest of the crew is swept away into the cargo holding area, he turns to the out-of-luck would-be hero and tells him to hide in their shared bathroom. When the patrol comes around, the Frenchman lies. Then, as the others are rounded up, well, he gets the man off the ship, doesn't he? He helps him to a lifeboat and tells him to get as far away as possible. He doesn't need to be told twice. So he does." The others looked on, interested.

"He's about halfway to the New Caledonian coast when the air- strike happens. That whole 'we don't negotiate with terrorists' thing. The ship sinks to the watery depths. It'll be a diving site in a few years with a story attached to it. Meanwhile the man makes landfall and finds himself a nice little bar. He sits down and explains what's happened to him. A woman along with a group of her friends listen to his story and what do you know it, she finds herself talking to him. They hit it off and he decides to stay in New Caledonia. He gets a job that he likes. They have a couple kids together. Happy endings for everyone who deserves it."

"lovely story!" The red words moved across the bubble-woman's face.

"What happened to his other wife?" Cherish wasn't impressed. "He just up and leaves her without a word?"

"I dunno. I guess everyone else thought he was dead. Maybe she got life insurance or something?" Young Heather shrugged in memory as she was trying to do in the present. It was a sarcastic gesture, her broad shoulders halfway to her head. She'd always been flexible, so this was hers alone – a way to cope in times of stress or boredom. It relayed a message to those around her that she was done with whatever was happening. Even if she happened to be the one to start it in the first place.

"Sometimes you don't need to tell everything," the old man said, easing himself to his feet using a cane for leverage. "Well, we'd better be going. If we don't get Margot's suit to a recharge station, her gel will start to get cloudy, and..." He stopped at that, held the thought, and continued. "It was wonderful to meet you kids. I hope your future is as bright as it can be! No. As it should be!" And with that, off the two went, hand in suit-sheathed hand.

"I've never seen a jelly bean that could talk before!" Timothy laughed. "Did you see the words appearing on her face? Man! It was like she was living inside a water mattress. Like... like a reverse scuba-suit!" He kept laughing.

The other two didn't laugh. At least, she didn't remember herself laughing. It was only a memory, and her present self could have easily contaminated it with the knowledge of what was waiting for her on the other side of the door. It swooshed closed and the doors ahead rushed open. Ahead, her eyes confirmed that the doctors were preparing a much more modern and slimmer model of GenCell's Cellular Preservation Suit®. She shuddered, squeezing her eyes shut for a long moment, hoping she would be drawn back again through the ages to a time when she was young and the world wondrous. This time, however, the Wilsons did not surface.

This time, she would not find consolation from her memories. She looked ahead at the CPS. It would provide her body with the means to keep the cellular replication process at bay. It would stop the cancer. It would lock her body in the state it was at this moment. Better even. She would be able to walk again. With practice, she would be able to run.

She would live, but was it really the life she wanted? Pride struck her. Humility embraced her. Vanity caressed her. And yet she chose to live. "We're ready to begin." The doctor, a man in GenCell vestments – royal purple and deep red – smiled and motioned her towards the encapsulation table.

She shrugged, shoulders momentarily reaching up to her ears, and went forward to lie down.

SIMPLETON

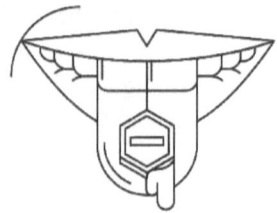

"So, what can you do?" The blonde bartender with brunette roots showing sipped her cocktail and leaned in further. "Come on. No need to be shy, hun. Look, lemme show you mine and then you'll show me yours, alright?" She slowly dipped her finger into the beer and looked up with a piercing gaze that demanded attention.

Maxime was unmoved, even as the liquid began to twist and twirl like a tiny alcoholic tornado. The amber whirlpool turned silently under its own power as the bartender's stare became a playful smile. Small miracles like this could no longer move the striking Asian woman, her thirty-some years having refined her cynicism to a knife's edge.

She shrugged at the bartender's grin, reached over and with a tug, promptly pulled the finger out.

"Please don't do that."

"Why not? It's fun, isn't it?" She put her head in her

hands. "Now. Tell me, stranger... What's your thing?"

Maxime shrugged. "I can't do anything." Her look turned to disgust as she watched the bartender, apparently without shame, lick her dripping finger. "Do you make a habit of going around finger-banging people's beverages?" She pushed her beer away. "Not the best way to keep customers, is it?"

"Sheesh. I wouldn't have done it if I thought you'd bitch like this. Fun people get a kick out of it." She sighed off the debate. "Look. Just tell me what you do, alright?"

Maxime leaned forward. "Nothing."

"Uh-huh. Right. Nothing's not a thing! Everyone here's got one." She looked at her still-drying finger, momentarily distracted, and then concentrated. "Come on, it was perfectly clean." Slowly, carefully, and with a practiced motion, the bartender traced a simple heart on the bar top, then smiled innocently.

"Look. We got off to a bad start. I get that. But, come on, look at this place. I'm bored." The bartender drew the word out with a smoky purr. "Just let me in already! I bet you've got a neat trick, don'tcha?" Maxime was rapidly losing her patience with the bartender. She tried a different tactic to restore the peace: old-fashioned awkward silence. Looking around, she hoped to catch the eye of someone nearby to drag into the spotlight. Her neck craned to scan the room, and spotted the only other patrons sitting in the corner booth. The couple kept to themselves, eyes locked together, whispering under the hypnotic beat of a song from before.

The turnout wasn't surprising, really. It wasn't a Friday or the weekend and given the hands on the clock, well, most people had better things to do than spend lunchtime hidden in a dive like this.

Maxime didn't. Who was to say what the real time was, anyway? Could a clock really be trusted in a bar without a name? Maxime wasn't sure – and her watch was set to the last place she'd been visiting, far and away.

Frankly speaking, she wasn't even certain what day it was. "Well?" The bartender was growing impatient. Maxime was still looking around, following the logic behind the vintage decor that was all the rage when the bar had probably been built. This low-tech motif didn't fly with the younger generation then, and that was still part of its appeal. Locations like this presented an opportunity for the surviving thirty somethings to get away from the craziness and immerse themselves in the nostalgia of wood paneling and frayed posters depicting movies and movements from when the world was very different – and less weird.

Simplicity was the key – the perfect pitch for someone trying to forget what the world had become.

Someone like Maxime. She looked towards the bartender, who was not giving up. "Fine. Let's see. Well, I'm not bad with computers. I can put together a real mean Excel spreadsheet if the pressure is on. I got pretty good at juggling, but that was back in my high school days, you know, before." She laughed in spite of herself as she remembered pelting friends and family with dubiously coordinated beanbags. "I'm pretty sure I could still do it if the situation called for it." She paused. "I'm not a bad cook, either."

"That's two! Do you have three talents?" Humored at last, the bartender's eyes were pools of delight.

"Not talents, no. More like hobbies. Well, not Excel, that's for work. I mean, who the hell would call working on spreadsheets a hobby? They'd have to be crazy. Right?"

"Could be. So you're not a... Technoton?" She pretended to type. "Nope."

"An Acroton?" She mimed a tiny backflip.

"No."

"How about a–"

"Nothing. Like I said before. Not a talented person, I guess. I really don't know what to tell you... What was your name?"

"Trrrrrisssta." She practically purred it out. Maxime nodded, glad to have introductions out of the way. "Alright. So, Trista, I'm getting the feeling there might be a bit of a miscommunication here. I'm not really into... uh... women?"

This didn't faze Trista half as much as Maxime had hoped it would. "Me either, but there's something about you. I felt it the second you walked in the door." She flashed a crooked but impeccably white smile. "Hold on." Without looking down, Trista reached behind the bar and pulled out a fresh, frothy pint that swayed from side to side as it came to rest near its half-finished, abandoned predecessor.

"There. All better, no?"

"I guess so. Still, I don't have anything to show you." Trista winked. "Not with that attitude! But maybe with a little push, we'll figure something out. Could be that it just hasn't manifested yet. Or you might just not know what you can do. I've heard of that before."

"Doubt it."

"I knew this one guy who was living in Washington State someplace where the Ni-Fi network wasn't very strong. Back before they set up the global metropolitan grid. He was like you, thought he didn't have anything special about him, then poof!" Her hands went up and as wide as her expression. "Suddenly he came into his talent. Bet you can't guess what he could do."

Maxime nodded and returned the bartender's smile, wondering whether this was a conversational technique or Trista actually expected her to guess. "I bet you'd be right!"

"Oh, come on. Don't be boring. Just humour me for a while, and the beer's on the house."

Maxime rolled her eyes. "Fine. Give me a clue at least?"

"Nope. Just name off the weirdest talents you'd ever heard, and if you get close I'll give you a little nudge in the right direction." She flashed that blinding smile again.

"Okay. Pyroton? Like, controls fire or whatever?" She watched Trista smirk. "What?"

"Oh, come on. You can think of weird stuff, can't you? Here, let me give you one example." She reached under the bar and placed it on the counter, cupping her hand over whatever it was so that Maxime couldn't see.

"So, I once had a guy who used to come in here. He would sit just over there." She pointed to a booth near the back of the bar where the lights were left on their dimmest settings. "Same order every time. Beer and peanuts. Then, without saying much of anything, he'd go back there and watch the tube. Rugby matches, mostly. So the first time he did it, I almost lost my shit. I'd be over here, serving a customer and out-of-nowhere you'd hear this odd clunk sound. Like... uh... a golf club hitting the side of his favorite Mercedes when you find out there's another woman." She held herself for a second. "Kidding. Still. Metal on metal. I thought something broke, so I walked over to investigate and, as I walked up, I saw him bite down on a peanut. Then, right there and then, poof – the peanut wasn't a peanut. It'd turned into this itsy-bitsy, teeny- weeny, little no-entry sign."

She lifted her hand to reveal exactly that. "Now, that was weird. Thing was, he didn't stop chewing on the peanuts. Apparently he could still taste and chew them, but he didn't dare swallow... I think you can imagine why. They might be no-entry, but they'd make a terrible exit, if you know what I mean." She ducked below the bar and promptly came back up. "Here." She held out another one and handed it to Maxime.

It was a two-centimetre large hexagonal sign with white contour, red background, and black lettering. Even the back had little bolt holes where you could have attached it to a signpost. The edges shined a brilliant chrome in the dull light.

They looked, by all accounts, like they had been made by tiny people to guard tiny doors or private Matchbox roads. Memories of reading Gulliver's Travels swarmed in Maxime's head. A well placed ad here or there, and a Lilliputian merchant might make a decent living off these oddities. Before the thought could be committed to long-term memory it was gone, stolen away as Trista leaned in only inches from her face.

"Go ahead, give it a smell." Trista smiled. Hesitant at first, Maxime obliged. "Oh, weird – it still smells like peanuts."

"Right! I thought it was pretty cute, actually. So I kept them around, you know, a souvenir or a – whatchacallit? – objet de memoire. I don't get out much, as you can imagine. Most of the people that come here are pretty much regulars." She paused. "Until they aren't. So, I have a few things – trinkets, videos, photographs, tiny no-entry signs, and all that. It's sort of like my own museum of oddities. A way to remember them. Things that you won't see again in a million years because those people don't come around anymore or were just passing through. I could show you later. It's in the back."

"You were asking me about the weirdest thing and I have to admit, this might well be it." She continued examining the sign.

"Right! Shoot. Okay, okay. I want you to guess what Tedd – that's the guy's name – could do." She smiled. "Think weird. Like. Really weird."

"Look, I really don't know. I'm not even a full beer in yet."

"Come onnnnn. Guess!"

"Fine. Whatever. Uh, could he make, uh, bath bubbles turn into seahorses?"

"Have you really met someone who can do that? Nooo waayy!" The way she said 'no' made it roll into the W sound at the end. "Though that does sound adorable."

"No. Just sounds weird."

"It does..." Her eyes considered it. "Could he... levitate if he was listening to Radiohead's song 'Creep'?" She did, in fact, know someone who had this talent. But during one flight, the CD skipped when it should have started over – a grim testament to the hazards of off-brand consumer electronics. He fell from a height of sixty-three feet onto Highway 132 after getting off a bus and trying to swoop over a particularly congested morning traffic jam.

"Nope." Trista said, missing out on one of Maxime's

favorite stories. "Well, could he talk to plants? Play music with cats? Turn himself turquoise? Did disco music come out of his ass when he farted? Walk through glass? Turn his voice into graffiti? Did he molt like a lizard or molt into lizards? I don't know, Trrrrrista! I give up!" Clearly, this game of throwing out random, half-imagined examples was exhausting Maxime beyond her capacity for afternoon whimsy.

Trista, on the other hand, was having the time of her life. "That's alright. At least you were trying this time! So, this guy–"

"Tedd." Maxime let out an exasperated sigh. "Yes, Tedd. He was in Washington State when all of a sudden he was standing naked next to his brother in Wisconsin."

"That's... yeah... you got me there. That's weird."

"No-no-no. It's not about that. It's about how he got there... Or why. Whatever – let me finish! So, he appeared next to his brother while he was mid-thrust and giving it to some bottled redhead in a motel room near their parent's place." She laughed. "The two of them were just a few years apart, but – well, you can imagine how they would have reacted. And that poor girl! They hadn't seen each other since GenCell announced Ni-Fi's secondary effects."

She thought for a second. "I can't really remember his brother's name... Anyway, for whatever reason, whenever Tedd or his brother were being intimate with someone, blammo! The other brother would appear right there in the same room not five feet from where the other, uh, finished. Now, the first few times it was pretty awkward, as you'd imagine, but the two of them made it work. Saved a lot on traveling costs."

Maxime hesitated. "When he was intimate or... any time?"

"You know the expression 'it takes two to tango'? Well, as it turns out, it takes two to teleport. Anyway, so I met Tedd one night and he explained that his brother needed a lift here and asked if I could lend him a hand, so to speak. Weirdest pickup line I've ever heard, but, well, I thought – this is just what I want to add to my little museum back there." She pointed again. "I got the whole thing on tape. I can show you later if you want. Tedd turned out to be a really polite guy. Proper gentleman and such. I miss him." She winked, through her eyes darkened for a moment. "But not his brother, ya know? He ended up being damn rude." She sighed, a little teary-eyed or just plain tired – Maxime didn't honestly care at that point.

"No. I think I'm good. Your description was... thorough."

"Oh, it's not pornographic or anything. More like an art piece. Like the peanut-signs."

"I'm sure it's great, but if you ask me to smell it, we're going to have a problem." She sighed and went back to her beer.

Trista was having enough of this. "Sheesh, I'm just trying to be friendly. This place gets quieter every day. If you're going to be coming around we might as well get to know each other, right?"

"Mmhmm. I guess." And then, realizing how she was acting, added. "No, I'm sorry. That was uncalled for. I appreciate the beer and the stories, but I'm just... having a bit of a rough time recently."

"Want to talk about it?"

"Not really."

There was a nice silence for a while, even though Trista was staring at her with the intensity of a star moments away from supernova; finally, incapable of containing herself, she broke it.

"That Ni-Fi, eh? Who'da thought it would fuck this place up so badly?"

"I don't know. It's always been pretty fucked. Now we just have some extra distractions and a little more mystery. I sorta like it."

"That's a good attitude." She poured her another glass, as Maxime had finished sometime during the Tedd story. "I don't know if I could keep myself positive if I turned out to be one of the only people that–" She stopped. "I don't mean... never mind."

"It's okay. Say it." She considered her next words. "I wonder what it is that makes you immune to the Ni-Fi... If you even are. I heard from this guy Bill Lambert, he worked at GenCell, that it's impossible for people to be completely immune. No one can resist forever. Eventually everyone exposed to the signal is changed by it."

"I don't know what to tell you. I literally just drove here from –" Trista clapped her hands suddenly. "Ever think that that's what your talent is?"

"What? Being a sim–" Trista cut her off with an abrupt "Don't use that word!" She shook her head and chuckled. "Sorry. Old habit. I forget that it's not really a bad word these days. I remember when people who weren't able to develop talents were shunned and mocked. Even a stupid one like mine got me... well, a lot of awkward propositions at work. But maybe that's why I've lived so much longer than the others. The cooler the feat, the less time you get to use it."

"It's a silly word, anyway." Maxime added. "Look at it this way. All of the rest of the people here, they get all these strange things that they can do, right? "Some of them are pretty nifty, like that man who predicts earthquakes or that girl who can cure diseases. You know, Saint What's-Her-Face. Then you... Then you have people like me – I can make beer spin, and even that's not guaranteed to please some people. I know it's at least kinda neat, but it's not like I can do it to a full bathtub or a swimming pool. Just a cup of beer. And only beer. Don't know why, but it gets me attention and tips, right?"

Maxime nodded. "Now, if we leave the Ni-Fi, what happens?"

"Withdrawal." She smiled. "That's a sweet way of calling it. Can we just call it what it is?"

Maxime sulked a little and said nothing. "Leaving the Ni-Fi... Well... We die." Trista's playfulness was gone. "Now, people like you, well, you're different, ain'tcha? You can leave the Ni-Fi grid anytime. You don't need the signal. You can go anywhere. You can go out to nature. You can just... go. We have to stay. We're...we're trapped, ain't we? Trapped in these fields, however long they bother to keep them up. How many people you reckon are like you? One in a million? Ten million? A hundred? Billions? Well, doesn't that make you special, too?"

Maxime smiled a little and shrugged. Their game was over, and there wasn't much left for her to say.

"And we... Well, the Ni-Fi doesn't let us live forever, does it? No. We're all dying. Some say only a few more years, couple decades at tops. Then we're all gone and the world is left to people like you. To clean up the mess we're all making." She waved goodbye to the twilit bar, now empty except for Trista.

"When Ni-Fi happened... this place was always full. We had to extend our hours to accommodate everyone. We had five bartenders behind here. Seven servers. Five cooks and a few busboys with a part-time runner for when we were really packed." Her waving hand stayed high and alert. "Now it's just me. Cooking, cleaning, and taking out the garbage. Now, it's just–" The thought was interrupted.

A couple walked in through the door at the back. The

man raised his left hand and a chair moved across the floor. He sat down and it moved him back to the table. The woman behind him laughed and laughed.

"We're the ones that got the shaft, so we might as well have some fun in the meantime. Don't take that away from us. You already have the rest."

It seemed clear that long after the rest of the world – from mountaintop settlements, to rural enclaves, to permanent seafaring colonies, to the corporate-owned orbital habitats – had moved on, those that remained would still be fighting shadows at noon. They were making the most of what had been forced upon them. Everyone had people they had already lost. People they had loved from the time before.

Trista lifted the warm pint she'd demonstrated her power on to her lips. "Cheers."

Maxime raised her own glass, at a loss for what to toast. "Cheers." There was a kinship between the two, something earned, yes, but something that existed beyond the circumstances of their meeting. They carried complementary spirits and seemed to recognize that within one another as their empty glasses found their ways back to the bartop.

Maxime reached out and hugged the woman on the other side. "You know, we're more alike than I was ready to admit... Tell you what. You take this."

Maxime handed over a slip of skin-coloured paper and placed it on the tabletop between them. It immediately drew in the colour around it, like a chameleon.

"Wow," Trista said. "I got it from a friend who, well... I... I'm sure you'll keep this safe. It means a lot to me. There won't be any more of these, you know?"

Maxime grinned and Trista smiled back, as bubbly as the moment they first met, taking the card and placing next to the no-entry sign, whose unmistakable coloration it mimicked perfectly.

Trista had a flash from the time before. Family. Friends. Things from an age long past. But as quickly as they had arrived, they were gone, replaced by the cold fact that time had little meaning here. Her people didn't live in the time before, and had no part to play in what came next. Theirs was a world that only existed now, and in many ways, that made it alright.

OUT OF SOURCES

"I don't really see why you're laughing about this. It's pretty damn serious. If they find out I helped you..." The caller was sour-voiced with a tone that reminded the man on the other end that while he wasn't in much hot water at work, he wouldn't hear the end of it after he got home.

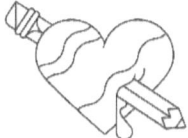

"Look. It's fine. Really. I just told Margot that it was all a misunderstanding and that I would take care in the future. I hate lying to people. And after I read the stuff, well, I didn't want her to think it was mine. No sense in justifying bad work, right? Anyways, she seemed fine with the whole situation."

"Uh-hnh. It's not about being lazy, Bill – it's the fact that you were caught. Now they'll have the interns sift through all your work and we'll have to deal with delayed payments. We have bills to pay. We have a kid on the way. You can't just do these things and expect to get off with a warning."

"My dear, lovely, wonderful, beautiful wife. It seems you're laboring under the delusion that they even care about what I write. You know how the programs work! I could spew lorem ipsum to my heart's content and I wouldn't hear so much as a murmur about it." He was smug, confident, and completely ready for this. Everything she hated when the two came to a tête-à-tête.

"Do you have any decency left, Bill? Any sense of shame about what you've done, and what you'll look like when they find out you've been fucking around like this? They'll lose respect for you. I've lost respect for you. Doesn't that count for something?"

"Calm down, Vera. You don't want the baby to inherit your special talent for shifting from love to hate in a split second."

"Fuck you. Dinner's at seven." She was about to hang up, but stopped short. "Don't be late."

"I won't."

"You better not. This is important. My parents have come in from–"

"I know, I know. We've gone over this a hundred times." His tone went flat. "Your father was an ex-military, grunt-type guy who owned a few assault rifles before the government took them away. Not the current one. That bad one that took over after his tour was finished. Your mother, well, she was from that country he went out to save." He struggled with his words. "What I'm trying to say is – would you mind lending me a hand with this?"

"Nope. I wrote it all down in that email you promised to review on the train back."

"Fine. Whatever. She was in that country. They met after he was wounded during a patrol. She was a nursing student who decided it was worth the risk to work with 'the enemy'. He was knocked out by an explosion and lost all hearing in his right ear." He paused to think and touched one side of his face and then the other. "No. I mean, his left ear. It turned out it was friendly fire and by the time he woke up from his surgery, well, he was a foot... I mean two feet, shorter." Vera didn't appreciate his attempts at stretched humour, especially when it involved someone she cared about. "So, don't mention his prosthetics. Don't stare at his facial scars. Don't ask about politics or foreign affairs." He exhaled and drew in a deep breath. "Ask about his favourite sports team. Ask about his gardening. Ask about the trip he and your mother have planned for the fall. Now, is that about right?"

There was soft, slow clapping on the other end, and what Bill could have sworn was laughter.

"Not bad. Not bad at all." He sighed in relief at that. "And last and most importantly?"

"Ask him if he would be so accommodating as to allow me to wed his dear, lovely, wonderful, beautiful daughter. Ask both of them. Say, how good is your mother's English?"

"Goodbye, Bill. See you at seven." The phone went silent and he leaned back in his chair, relaxed and confident once more. Ahead of him, glaring like a lighthouse locked in a staring contest with the wide, unwelcoming ocean, was the unopened email from his boss, whose telltale words did not bode well for his future. The future he had intended to spend with his dear, lovely, wonderful, beautiful wife and their indeterminately-sexed baby. He would have appreciated knowing what gender the child was, you know, to prepare, whereas she was more interested in adding mystery.

"When we were young," she explained the night when he begged her to let the ultrasound technician reveal the details, "there was so much we didn't understand. Most kids are curious, but I could almost feel the gaps in what I knew. Every new fact and experience made me feel... well, more whole, and so I kept asking questions. Now, my parents loved Christmas. I know you were never into it, but you have to understand that for my brother, my sister, and me, it was exciting enough to make you piss your pants. And of course I had to know what I was getting. But we were always told that if we were patient, we would find out that those boxes contained exactly what we hoped for. This is why I want to keep it a secret. Because the truth is, the more I learned about the world, the more I had to fear. The world is fragile, Bill. It's cruel. But this – I want to know this more than anything, and that's exactly why I need to wait. So let me have this one thing. Please?" And she always got what she wanted, didn't she? He looked at the screen ahead and gave it a daring click. Hoping that he had been too fast for the infernal machine to make sense of what he'd done.

"My office. Now," was all he needed to see. He glanced at the timestamp. It had arrived forty-five minutes ago.

Sighing, Bill stood up and went out the door. His office had the almost-honorific title of 'Head Content Developer' with his name, B. Burroughs, embroidered on a small sheet of laminate on the otherwise bare, green-blue door.

All the office was green-blue. It was the company's motif and it carried throughout – and not just the paint. The upholstery and the company uniforms; the window tints and the light fixtures. It was almost like being under a calm Caribbean ocean. He felt a little like a fish as he moved through schools of people speaking amongst themselves about this project and that anecdote. Someone almost stopped him, a woman he knew quite well, but he waved her away with his right hand and a look of despair that cut to the point.

Ahead, the purple door awaited. It was intentional, of course. The colour. It gave the place a disconnected, segregated feel. When you got called in there you knew it could only be for a great, if not terrible, purpose. Lives were made in the room beyond. Lives were ripped open and left exposed in a way that almost assured you would find yourself working at a local Stop-'N-Go for the rest of your meagre existence. People would die for his job; people had probably killed for it. The heaviness of Bill's worry made him feel like the ground was going to swallow him up. Still, he reached forward and went to turn the handle and meet his destiny.

It creaked open. Again, intentional. It would have been an easy task for a custodian or a junior member of the team to fix. But none dared fix it without permission. And none dared ask.

"Good timing." Margot's voice sounded calm and secure. "I was about to send Michelle to fetch you. Now, sit down." The room was as you'd imagine: purple-on-purple with a gold lining that, for those familiar with their alcohol brands, looked downright regal.

He obeyed. There was a silence. Intentional. As Margot Larein was known for. Everything came down to meaning and purpose. Everything and everyone fit into her world like clockwork.She wasn't merely powerful – she was a bona fide pioneer who transformed a third rate blogging site into an algorithmically-generated news feed that served billions. Some said her insights into natural language processing and narrative cognition made her a modern Turing.

She was a beautiful difference engine. Bill hated her as much as he wanted to worship her.

"Look, Marge, I know what you've probably heard and I just want you to know that I was just experimenting with an idea."

Her head tilted to the side, calculating. "I wanted to see if people really are following the content the way we wanted. I just didn't think it was going to turn into such a scandal."

"Sssscannndal?" She said smoothly. "No. I don't think we have a scandal on our hands here, William. I did, however, believe that I had hired a Burroughs, not a Borrower." He smiled at that. He had to.

"Ah, but you think I am attempting to be funny?" Her face was crossed with glaring ridges that made her into the epitome of a Disney villain. "I'm not trying to be funny. I'm serious. We don't have a scandal. What we have is a complete breakdown of protocol. What I can't abide is knowing that a member of my hand- picked staff is going against our company's fundamental ethos and paying for others to create content that he is entirely capable, if not even overqualified, to write himself."

He was holding back a wall of emotions. In a few weeks it would mark his seventh year working in the green-blue office. Five spent in the trenches paying his dues, and two that had seen a respectable raise and benefits. Benefits he was going to need for...

"Vera is pregnant!" Bill blurted out. This did not surprise his employer. "Look, I'm sorry for outsourcing those articles. I won't let it happen again. I just... I had all these things to do and had to find a new place with room for a nice nursery. I went looking for nannies, because we both work and the baby will need someone to take care of it. I had to learn all this stuff about crap. Literally. I had to read books on what certain types of crap mean and how you should react. I went to these courses and now I'm all jumbled up because I don't know what to do and if I even want this to happen anymore. Please, you have to understand that this was a once-in-a-lifetime mistake!" The tears were flowing easily now. She was smiling.

"You may be a colossal idiot but I'm not about to fire you, Bill. I enjoy our chats and you have, despite this one occasion – and it had better only be one occasion – never disappointed me. I want you to take some time off. In fact, there are two men here that wanted to speak to you about where you were getting that content. Naturally, after I read it, I knew that it couldn't be you who had put it together." She turned her computer screen around. "I mean, did you even edit these, Bill? They're dreadful. I mean, really." She made a sound of disappointment that rang in his head.

"Two men? What do you mean?" Margot looked at her nails, fancy as always, and leaned back in her purple armchair. "I didn't ask after they showed me their badges."

Bill swallowed. "Badges?"

"From a very secretive government branch, I'm told. I called a few of my friends and so far as I can tell, they are entirely legitimate. I told them to leave their guns outside the room, though. I'd rather you not be put in a position where you might soil yourself after that great cry, you big baby." She was all smiles and affection again. The effect was chilling.

"Well? They should be in your office by now. I had Freric search them, so you'll be as safe as he wants you to be. I hope you gave him a nice gift for his birthday last month, that's all I'm saying." She motioned her hand to shoo him away and before he had fully realized what had happened, he was back in his office with two men in gray, striped suits. They were difficult to look at. The moment you thought you'd found something that was reflective of personality or individuality was the same moment that your attention drifted over to the other and the impression restarted. One had a thin nose and the other, well, it was squished up against his face. Both had brown eyes and both, upon entering, motioned him to where he now was sitting in a synchronicity that felt about as awkward to watch as it was to obey.

Neither introduced themselves or provided credentials, though Bill could see empty creases in their suits where one might have a gun holstered.

"Bill," Fat Nose started. "We hear you've been

paying someone to do your work for you."

"It's true," he admitted. What was the point in lying now? "We need to know who that person is," Thin Nose continued, "where they are, and how you originally found them."

"I can look at our correspondence. It shouldn't be hard to figure it all out. As for where – well, I just posted an anonymous job on a writing community board and this person was the first to respond. I didn't really care about quality. I just wanted to have time to get my life in order."

Fat Nose typed the details into his jet-black smartphone. "We've already looked into your accounts, Bill. Whomever you were in touch with has been very thorough in covering their tracks." He shrugged. "We've got some pretty impressive resources at our disposal, so you can appreciate that we're a little concerned that we have no details or trail to follow."

'Gone?' He mused on that for a moment. "I don't think I follow, unless you mean that somehow this other writer got in and erased our emails.

"Not just the emails. Your payment records. Your posts on the community site – yes, we knew all about that – and by the time we started to put two and two together, it was all simply gone."

Fat Nose sat on the edge of the green desk. "We can't tell you much, Bill. But we want you to know about our suspicions, just in case you happen to receive any follow-up from this... person." He leaned in a little, blocking the ceiling light. "We believe whoever wrote your content for you was placing secret messages. Plans. Locations. Dates and times. We think..." He turned to Thin Nose, who nodded.

"We believe this is the terrorist cell that was responsible for the massive friendly-fire incident in – well, I don't need to remind you about what happened, do I? When communications broke down, and all those people turned on one another because their superiors delivered conflicting orders."

"But, you can't mean... That was almost thirty years ago."

"We have our reasons. We think they've fine-tuned their methods and they've been slowly growing a presence on native soil. This was the closest we've been to catching up with them, and we need you to be ready and willing to give us your full attention and assistance should you be approached by anyone related to those posts." Thin Nose was pacing around the room.

"If they're moving this fast... We can't have a lot of time, Bill. They could spring their little trap at any point and, well, if we're being honest with you, we haven't had a good whiff of anything in a clean decade. Sure," he waved his hands in the air, "we should be pleased that nothing's going on." His head cocked forward. "The chaos from their last operation never fully faded. People are still suspicious. New copycat groups – not nearly as sophisticated, but still dangerous – spring up every day. These people are smart. Smarter than me.

Smarter than you. Smarter than everyone in this damn
turquoise office. You understand me, don't you?"

He nodded. "Yes. You'll be the first to know if
anything happens. Just tell me how."

Thin Nose handed him a SIM card. "Put this in your
phone and dial 1-2-4-3. It might not be an elegant passcode,
but it's one you'll remember. Won't you, Bill?"

"Yes."

"Good. Well, it's about quitting time, ain't it? We've
asked your boss to give you a few days to recover. Hopefully,
someone will get in touch with you before then. If not, count
yourself lucky, man. Count yourself lucky and we'll never
cross paths again. Just know that even if this all seems
unlikely, you're our best chance to get these guys. Got it?"

"Got it." He was stuck in a loop, and when the agents
left he couldn't stop thinking about what the hell he had just
learned. It wasn't hard for him to figure out who was
responsible for the content that he'd so graciously and
thankfully placed online. In all the confusion and the
craziness, his mind had clued in immediately. Now, the
question was: Why? Why would she do it? Little lines
connected. It was her family. Her father, who had been
wounded out there during that terrible page in history. Her
mother, born in the chaos of war.

It was a family operation, or it was just the woman
who shared his bed. And Bill was late for dinner with all of

them.

The Program

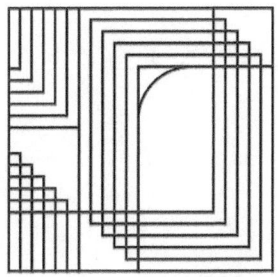

WHAT
WASN'T
SAID

Is it
millennia of
evolution or simple
force of habit that
has ensured that, no
matter how much
we try to fight it,
that sleep is more
difficult in the open air than in the comforts of a warm, soft
bed – shielded from nature's light and its cut through the slime
layer of skin between dreams and reality? And why don't we
have thicker eyelids? That, for the moment, would help.
Anything to help me sweep up the pieces of that dream, the
last night I'll be able to believe it.

I keep my eyes closed. I pray that the sun will have
pity. I want to sleep. I beg for fantasies, no matter how
outlandish, to rip me from my life.

Epiphany strikes me and, keeping my eyes sealed, I
reach around for a blanket or pillow to put up a more durable
barricade to soften the impact of the events of the night before.
My hands come up empty.

I'm not sure where I am, and I'm not really ready to
find out. No matter how sincere the negotiations I attempt with
reality, no matter how I bargain, I am left with only one

recourse: I have to get up.

Master of your own body, my ass. It shouldn't come
as a great shock to awaken this damaged. Last night marked
the ten year anniversary of the day my ex-wife, Jean – we
were married back then – up and decided to become part of
the Program.

You must remember those old commercials, the ones
that started with that cute couple looking over the New
Bethlehem skyline. That little spot that they focus on in the
distance marking the dividing wall between the countryside
and the Aggregated New York Megapolis. If you don't, you're
probably too young to realize how hard we fought against the
transition back then.

Now it has become standard. Necessary. Trendy. I
can't get over the way the man in the ad looked at his wife,
how a perfectly romantic moment blossomed into a sick
caricature of happiness. They reached out and just as their
hands touched, they turned to the camera and blissfully asked
us to "Be a part of the solution. Get with the Program."

If you don't remember them, well, like I said, you
were born after the civil protests quieted down and our leaders
were silenced – one way or another. These days, they're in
every content stream. Not those actors specifically, but that
same smile, and that same message. Do what we say. We
know best. Make choices that you have every goddamned
right to refuse.

I like to think that neither of the people in that
vintage propaganda piece actually believed what they said,

because it makes me feel better about my own decisions. I find myself sick to my stomach wondering if Jean actually bought into it like so many others across the world. That she believed the company line. I mean, sure, the incentives were attractive, but to lose that part of what you are – the potential you can offer the world – seemed to me then, as it does now, to be a fundamental betrayal of what it means to be human.

It seems so obvious these days what it all meant for us, but skeptics like me learned that silence meant safety.

I was twenty-seven when I returned home to find Jean smiling at the door to our condo on the Upper E-End near the coastal barricade. She was excited in a way that I had never seen before and because of that I absently allowed myself to get pulled into the gravity of the moment.

"I did it!" she said to me, holding out the freshly-stamped slip of Causal Paper (or Causper) that they were so reluctant to let any of us E-Enders get a hold of. It was practically in the bylaws that we had to ask permission before moving forward. I did my best to keep a smile on my face. "We're going to be just fine." Jean was referring to our recent tax problems.

I was on a part-time shift out in the Farming Tower in Brisbane and she, well, there wasn't much call for technical assistants when she graduated from the Kong Academy at thirty-two. I mean, I couldn't blame her for her education decisions; everyone needs a degree. If you got caught without one in E-Ender (or any of the Ender buildings across the boundless cityscapes of America), you got shipped out to one of the unaffiliated settlements (like one of those independent floating fiefdoms).

There was a time when we thought – well, that they were basically prison camps. But as I've personally experienced, that rumour is mostly untrue. Mostly.

I can remember taking the Causper, gut filling with dread and fear, wondering what Jean had done to earn it. There were only so many ways a person could be guaranteed a place in a Megapolis, and of all the ones I knew, only one surfaced. Darkly.

"You didn't!" I tried to hold back my emotions, but they all exploded at once – first uncertainty, then anger, and finally fear. "What do you mean by that?" Her face inverted itself. "It's my body. I can do what I want with it."

I wasn't caught off-guard by this, but I let my anger make the point badly. "I wasn't suggesting that I should have any control over your body, Jean. I was just–"

"Just what? We needed this, Tim. I mean, isn't this what you want? To stay here in our lovely little home and be close to our lovely friends? Your father? My mother?" She had this all planned, I had no doubt.

"Stop it. I don't want to argue. I just... I thought this would be a decision we could make together. I mean, what would have happened if you arrived home after a long workweek and found out that I'd... that I had gotten with the Program?"

She scoffed. "You're still on about that old ad? It's not about fitting in anymore. I did this for the future."

"Not our future." I tried not to sound melodramatic but failed miserably.

"We knew what this was. I assumed we did at least. If you had any complaints, you should have stated them in our marriage agreement."

"I mean... I didn't, but I still thought that these were things we would be able to talk about before one of us just jumped ahead and did it!" I went from calm to yelling in a heartbeat. It came from somewhere primal, a cornered animal that knew only anger and betrayal. But as righteous as my fury was, it couldn't silence the small voice inside that agreed with her.

"I don't believe this! We couldn't afford one even if we wanted to." Her arms went wide. "And I never said I wanted one." Her finger pointed right between my eyes. "You would never be able to afford one, either – and I sure as hell won't be stuck supporting all three of us." She started towards the parlour. I followed, but I could see that forgiveness wasn't going to come easily for me, if at all.

New York's spacescrapers were twinkling in the dimming light behind her.

"I did this for us," she said. "We only had a few more credit points left and then, well, what would you have us do? Move to the colonies or the farms if we refused to leave

Earth?"

I sat down. "I don't know. I just wanted you to let me be part of the decision." I looked to my feet and felt about as low as I thought possible.

Things didn't improve from there. Fights turned into full-blown marital warfare that fired on all frequencies. In the end, Jean opted for a dissolution based on incompatibility. She claimed her points from joining the Program, and within five months, I was evicted from our sunny spot on the one-hundred and seventeenth block of Fairfield Towers.

I found myself in New Bethlehem after that, working the same job and maintaining myself but empty inside.

Ten years it's been. I think about her often. Today is one of those days that my hypocrisy comes 'round full swing, and I can feel a lifetime's worth of self-disappointment at once – as though all those memories have come to life and, in a chorus, are screaming at me now.

Decisions that have marked each and every day of my life. Today, though, there is something else missing. No – something has been taken, and the cornered animal that roared to save it in Fairfield is back. Only this time, it's screaming at me.

A flurry of images come back. Slowly, inevitably, the neural implant that captured the events is stitching the memories across the black spaces that the synthexahol created.

It went like this: I was out with the others from our weekly meetings, drinking away time. Long hours of hard work marked off with sips of technically illegal but surprisingly affordable mind-altering beverages, consumed in dingy dive bars that could have passed for a Prohibition-era speakeasy, if it weren't for the monitors.

These friends-against-convention and I laughed and watched the NeuroNet elections as new Government One policies went from concept to law.

Did we miss Order 22, or was it intentionally kept from us? I don't really know. I want to think I would have fought against it if I had known what it really was. Politics, eh? At 12 midnight on February 6th it went live. They'd already rigged New Beth's filtration systems for it, and that's where I get skeptical about whether we had ever been free. If our thoughts mattered at all, or if they had always been too heavy to reach the top of Tower One, where the President and his cabinet of genofuturists dreamed of a nation that went to sleep one way and...

I awaken with the notification at the end of the playback, flashing like a firefly in the front of my mind. Like an old petroleum-powered vehicle that's running out of fuel. Like a tell- tale digital clock begging to be reset after a power outage.

With only small accommodations made to those with exceptional influence and power – and understand that this means an almost immeasurably tiny number of very special people – none were spared from the final draft into the Program.

There will never be another that shares in the genes I had to offer. There will be humans under Government One, but with Eugenics Order 22 in effect, only those favoured few will ever have the pleasure and the privilege of producing offspring. The morning of February 7th, we enter a brave new world where humanity takes an unprecedented step towards sustainability... and yet all I can ask, selfishly, is what my son or daughter would have looked like if only life had been fair and nature true.

I think, selfishly, what life might have been if I had chosen this fate back when Jean had tried to convince me it was the right thing to do.

Was I not human enough?

THE DAYS

Miranda looked at the dial ahead of her, obscured by condensation from recycled breath and sweat. It gave her a 10 minute window before the caustic atmosphere outside found its way into her lungs. Her instincts told her the sensors must be broken, because it smelled like that had already started. Something had to be broken, or she hoped that was the case – because it would be an understatement to say the smell in the cabin wasn't already reaching her personal limit.

Moments like this forced her to consider whether it was worth the paycheck. Not that there was a whole lot of opportunities considering the state of, well, States back home.

What was it that Emersong said after L-Day? That this was the twilight of the human empire. That the dawn was far and away. That the world was due for its next dark age.

Was this it? Asphyxiation aside, this was one of the better options, if not the best, that someone without a degree or a commission from the Program could hope for.

She placed a tab of synthetic mood – a Symood – under her tongue and plugged the ridge of her nose with a painful, though effective hair clip.

"Shit!" A ship grew large on the viewport as it careened through the clouds at dangerous speeds. She threw her hands to the left, detached from her tethered course, and narrowly avoided the vehicle heading in the opposite direction.

"Asshat." She spat and logged the event before coupling back to the original flight plan. At the end of day, Venus wasn't all that bad if you discounted the sulfuric weather patterns and the tendency for the thermometer mercury (not to be confused with the planet where Miranda had one unfortunate friend stationed) to go up as far as 460 °C. She wasn't getting a tan here unless she wanted to be barbecued or frozen in the process.

Okay, well, maybe it did suck a little being on Venus. She wondered why the old myths associated Mars with men and war. The metaphor holds up at first; with its harsh, rusted appearance, the Red Planet was a stark contrast to the bright golden colours and light blues of Venus. But with corrosive air and scorching heat, the real war was here, and Mars was a veritable paradise in comparison. The Martian terraforming trials would only take a few generations of carefully-timed carbon bombs and polar melts, whereas Venus... Yeah. We'd never stop fighting her.

The comm flared to life. "Do you have any last requests?" Commandant Waller asked with a tone that suggested he couldn't care any less about her answer.

"Just get me the numbers for the lottery, Jules."

Not going to win."

"A woman can dream."

"Can you? News to me. Do you want anything to eat? The Market will be closed by the time you've landed and gone through Contamination Control."

"I've got some snacks in my bunk. I'll pick stuff up tomorrow."

"Believable! Just... totally and entirely believable. Every-damn- time. I ask you every time and you always have some answer like that. Are you a squirrel? Where are you keeping all these goodies?"

"Nowhere. Just forget you heard anything about my treasure, you pilfering pig. And if you think I'm prepared to share with you, Grasshopper, well, you'd have a much better chance of winning the lottery. This ant works hard for her creature comforts. Plus, I just don't need much."

"Alright Aesop. I'm just surprised to hear you plan to eat at all. I thought you closed your eyes, plugged in, and recharged like the Billybots."

"Har-har."

"Nothing else then?"

"Not this time, thanks. Say, can you tell me who was casting down a few minutes ago? They were using my line to get to the worksite. I almost had a head-on collision."

"Only other operator in your sector right now is Alvar."

"Him? Christ, I thought you were firing him! Preferably into open space, if you're taking suggestions."

"I was. Got a notice from Foreman Quilt. Apparently the kid's got some pretty deep connections, and they'd rather have him here to be our problem than to deal with him themselves."

"Pissant bourgeois incompetents... No understanding of the proletariat. It's no wonder our society is falling apart."

"Watch it."

"Bah, you're about as Bourg as you are skinny."
Waller's laugh echoed across the comm. "Alright, Miranda.
That's enough for now. I'll see you after you get through the
scrubbers." The line went dead a moment later and Miranda
went back to carefully piloting through the heavy sulfur
clouds. As expected, they were already wearing through the
outer hull. Bits of the exo-shell dripped off of it in a stream of
partially realized vapour. She squinted, which was
unnecessary with a polarized window that blocked the intense
Venusian light and kept her retinas from baking.

Hard to fight one's own nature, though. A sign
appeared on the viewscreen that signalled she'd reached the
upper limits of the Class S miner's flight capabilities. Much of
the fuel tank had been damaged during a previous shift when
the ship was attacked by marauders, reducing its operating
range.

The others had not been so fortunate. None of this,
however, was information Miranda had been entrusted with.

They weren't meant to know about the war. Or what
fate was casting a shadow across time, back to them. The ship
would need repairs, which was fairly common, so why should
she be expected to ask questions? The Billybots would get to
that as soon as they retrieved the ore from the mining camp at
Venera Co. Site Thirteen.

Something shimmered against the scenic background
of the blazing sun. Miranda smiled, knowing she was almost
free from the suffocating aromas that were nearly coming to

life in the back of her mouth. She set the autopilot, eased her line, and transferred the data through the Stream to the archive on the Aarth- Clan Cloudrunner. It was appropriately named, for a station, hovering above the calamity below. Like a pebble in the sky. It was home, too. That's what mattered to her most – and when it was in sight, her muscles relaxed and her feelings of discomfort seemed to melt off her body like so much exo-shell.

She landed and disrobed, and was cleaned, decontaminated, and through the scrubbers in just under twenty-five minutes. It was a record that suggested (to those entitled to such facts, at least) that the Billybots had finished their repair rounds, and had moved on from the vital systems that had been damaged during the last siege.

Standing at the entrance to the commons, Jules presented her with a plate of cooled food and a smile on his face.

"Look, I know what you said, I just didn't want to risk you getting sick just because you're too damn stubborn and trying to save a few bucks for that trip back Earth-side."

Miranda took it without complaint. "I want to see my kids. It's been... years."

"I remember. Jean must be in her thirties now."

"Something like that."

"Has she found anyone new?"

"Not since she left Tim. He was a nice guy but, well, you know what Earth is like under those dick Genarchists. They want everyone to fit into their paradigm." She held out her hand. "Do you have a smoke?"

"Really?"

"Yes, fucking really. I almost got myself splattered because some novice piece-of-crap wasn't paying attention to his casting line. I need to relax."

"You could just use a mood stabilizer."

"Could, and did. That was practically why it happened. I didn't have my nerves ready to deal with the situation." Jules looked her over and sighed, giving in to her demands.

"When is the next shipment arriving from HQ?"

"It was scheduled for next cycle, but between you and me, I've been hearing rumours of raids across the planet. I swear, if we can't get those freelancers in line, we're going to have a full-out war on our hands – and I don't want to clean up the Commission's mess."

"Bourgs, Genarchists, and freelancers are all setting pretty shitty examples for the next generation." Miranda lit her smoke and sat down with the plate of food on her lap. "I swear, the last century has proven the point for people who went on the Nexodus."

"They're not going to be settling anything for another... I don't know how long... but that generation ship is no better, I can bet you." Jules sat down next to her. "We've got to get our hens in order today and then we'll focus on what to do tomorrow, right?" Miranda blew the purple smog out of her lungs, and filled her mouth with a piece of vatsynth chicken. She shrugged at the point. "Did you consider my proposition?" He leaned in and rubbed his nose against her full cheek. "If we were to bond formally we could get a nice little bungalow on the aft deck, probably get a few options for parenting. Wouldn't you like to actually be around for your..." He stopped, thought hard, and retraced his words. "Wouldn't you like to give your kid everything you can offer without worrying that some government fuck is lurking around the corner waiting to pick her up, draft her into the Academy, and convince her to join that damned Program?"

"Dat wouf b'e ice." Pieces of the synthetic food hit Jules in the eye. Miranda swallowed with a playful smile. "Look, it's not like I didn't fight to get her back. I just wasn't credible back then."

"Well... You are now. I could vouch for you, and we could start our own life here. Together." He smiled. She was at least twenty real-years older than Jules, but the way the rejuvenation treatments worked she could have easily been his daughter. Some people just didn't respond as well to the process.

"I won't lie. I want exactly that. I just can't shake the feeling that I left things rough with Jean. I didn't get to see her during those developmental years and when they let us reconnect in her teens, well, she was so different and they were really pushing the backlash against bio-parents..."

"Brainwashing is a bitch."

"No. I was the bitch. I could have gone back and finished my degree and they would have at least let me see her. I was just... lazy. She knows it. I know it. You know it."

"That doesn't matter out here. The corps want us to have kids."

"Then what? They grow up and pilot the next wave of gas or mineral seekers. What kind of life is that? They'll never be allowed on Earth. They'll never know the feeling of grass under their feet. That's not what I want for our kids. For all the things I did wrong, at least Jean got the chance to breathe real air on a real planet." She placed her hand on Jules'. "I didn't mean any offence. I love everything you are. I just... If you could watch the seasons change, feel the rain on your face... you would understand what I miss every minute I'm out here. It's home."

He wasn't offended. There was a lot to find beautiful about Venus. It was different, sure, but in the same way Miranda was incapable of appreciating Venus like a native, so was he unable to accept her image of Earth as the true meaning of "home".

"If you need to go back..." He sighed. "I'll help you in any way I can. Just be sure that you don't get yourself too caught up that you won't come back to me, eh?" His smile was sincere and he reached for the smoke.

"Do you think I could convince her to come here?

Could she come here and start a family, too? It would be weird at first, but maybe we could make the connection we never had during her childhood as we raised children side by side." It was an odd concept, but not entirely unheard of on the floating cities. Lifespans were routinely lengthened to well over a century, thanks to technology like the CPS and telomere extension treatments. It was expensive at first, but a healthy, perpetually youthful workforce was in everyone's interest. The Venusian corps understood the need to provide family support, because while longevity wasn't a problem, there was a growing mortality rate to contend with among surveyors, miners, and the new (and sorely needed) crop of Interceptor pilots. Not that many people knew about them.

"I will support you with whatever you feel you need to do." Jules let out a puff of purple air. It wasn't nicotine-laced. It was essentially vapour at this point, but the sensation still helped stave off real addictions to harder pharmaceuticals like mood stabilizers.

Miranda smiled, thinking of her daughter across the stretch of space, content that they were going to spend that dream-future together. She couldn't have known what was looming around the corner.

Outside the effective radar range of the Cloudrunner, the freelancer mining ship attached itself to the station's starboard cast line. War was not so far away after all.

"I'll start to draw up the –" Jules was cut off by an impact somewhere far away but close enough that he was thrown across the floor, tumbling through debris and bodies blown in from the hallway. Buckling as its suspensor fields failed, the Aarth-Clan's sole habitat plummeted through the sulfur clouds. Sirens blazed. Screams were muffled. Thrusters fired.

The lights flickered out and the smell Miranda had been so eager to escape swam through her nostrils and clogged her throat. She would never have the chance to learn about her daughter. She would never get to bring more lives into the world or watch them grow. Down they went, like a ship of old Earth caught in a great tempest. As a thousand souls winked out of existence, Miranda realized something – that no matter what faction claimed responsibility for her death, and no matter how the Commission responded, Venus would always win in the end.

THE SPAN

THE WANDERING WORLD

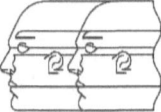

"Sereh would have appreciated this. It's a shame she decided to retire. I ask myself, though, would she be capable of laughing in the face of this one? You know, like she always claimed she could. Would she have been able to look over True Law 12.3B and know what to do here? If we had listened to her more closely... would he have found a loophole to apply? Gods be damned, it's almost ironic, really." He waited. "Hello? What, no pithy comment this time?" A symphony of crickets would not have been uncalled for. Or perhaps a tumbleweed rounding the corner and making its way across the blue-tinted floor. He imagined the march of a chirping chorus accompanied by the gentle brush of a tumbleweed, the strains of an impossible orchestra echoing slightly as it processed out of the Emergence Chamber.

None of that happened. Auxiliary-Ceras was speaking to himself, figuratively and literally, what with his Primary on the other end ensuring that the transfer was a clean, uncontaminated one. For most people this may have seemed unusual, but for Ceras, both versions of him, it was well within his understanding of 'normal'.

The version of himself that manifested here was not surprised, then, that the hyperfeed remained quiet. "We're good, aren't we?" the Auxiliary-Ceras sighed, wondering if his Primary had somehow taken offense at his need for reassurance.

While it was not surprise that he felt, it was certainly a species of disappointment. There aren't many occasions when you can find out what you really think of yourself. But the Council didn't care much for those types of conversations. And time was running out.

"What I am trying to say is that we are in a predicament that leaves very little room for error." The Crusade ship, having received its orders the moment Aux-Ceras had been born, had already set a course and was en route to the destination now. Its ferromorphic hull had seamlessly exchanged the insignia of the Continuous Realms, which carried its share of political baggage, for the red and gold ensign of Kilgore, Ceras' home sector and one with a neutral standing toward the parties in question.

His trip, deemed a priority for interspatial politics, meant he was allowed to use the DeepString to skip the years of travel that conventional craft would require. This came at considerable expense to the Council but ensured an audience in mere hours, Earth Standard Time (EST), with the opposition's arbiter – a renegade whose reckless defiance, if the rumors were true, could threaten civilization itself.

It was, however you cared to look at the situation, in the best interest of the Realms to resolve the issue quickly and with as little wasted energy, beyond this specific allowance, as possible. The Council's most trusted agents could not be ignored. Although the specifics varied in each report, something was about to happen, and nothing had served the Realms better over the millennia than vigilance.

Somewhere, back near Old Earth, Ceras Prime had probably been excused from the DeepString transfer centre. He was probably on his way to have dinner or something, trying to keep from doing too many things so as to keep his mind relatively clear for a clean reintegration later on.

Again, standard procedure for the use of Parallels like Aux-Ceras. When the assignment was completed to the satisfaction of the Council, they would only need to clip the DeepString on the Auxiliary's end. Then, this consciousness would be carried back across the curvature of space, flowing within the Span.

In a short while, this incarnation of Ceras would be subsumed into the dominant Primary along with all memory of its journey – and the fewer experiences the Primary had in the meantime, the less of a hassle it would be to sort out and integrate the Auxiliary memories.

Utilizing the DeepString, however, required payment. Orchestrated with careful consideration and mathematical precision elsewhere in the Realms to offset the cost that supraluminal travel would otherwise incur. A payment in energy. A convenience tax. The principles underpinning the exchange were quite sound and understood – but also, without special permission from the True Justice himself, quite illegal. With punishment in the form of permanent death.

After all, relativity would demand balance. Every civilization had different ways of settling the tab, as it were. The Ghora simply refused to decelerate outside of dense dark matter fields, although early enthusiasm for the technique had severely depleted the clouds of their home sector, guaranteeing that all but the most important craft made one-way trips. The vanguard wardrones of the Drathi turned FTL equalization into a weapon, typically destroying a gas giant or two to send gravitational shockwaves (and rogue moons) through their enemies' solar systems. And the generation ships of the Lauphrey were designed with such unimaginable redundancy that 90% of the craft's mass (crew included) could be subsumed into energy with negligible impact on spaceworthiness or the colonists' genetic diversity. But these were all localized phenomena limited by the crass demands of conventional spacecraft design. Only the Continuous Realms and its closest allies could use the Span to its fullest potential. All that an agent of the Realms needed to travel within the Span was the sanction of the True Justice, cooperation from the Bank, and a friendly ship with a DeepString transceiver and matter synth on the other end. That, and a healthy enthusiasm for sending a copy of one's consciousness across the vacuum of space.

The Continuous Bank had plotted the equalizing event for this specific trip somewhere near the edge of the Eastern Arm Expanse, nearest to where the Span touches the Shatter. Uninhabited by any starfaring race, unsuited for sublight travel – in short, astronomically insignificant. It had been chosen through an n-dimensional flowchart of Commissioned Powers and due process, and all the legal and philosophical terms that helped reconcile humanity with the esoteric principles of Alt-Physics. It was a process that had been written into the Amendment. Any use of the DeepString was meticulously documented.

The reach of the True Justice was so complete, and DeepString technology so closely guarded, that vanishingly few made the journey without his personal approval. It was difficult, despite the Realms' vast computational resources dedicated to calculating the cost of DeepString use, to accurately predict how much the universe would ask for in exchange for tricking it into doing the impossible.

You can't really negotiate with the universe.

Yes, it is complicated. Yes, it is strange. It is a whole slew of other things more troubling than that. There is little doubt that even a carefully moderated panel of the technicians, scientists, and bankers responsible for Aux-Ceras' two-way trip across the Span could even begin to provide a comprehensive explanation for how or why the process worked.

But there it is. It works! So, on rare occasions like this one, the leader of the Continuous Realms of Humanity, the True Justice, made... alterations to the areas within the Span and voila here he was, halfway across the galaxy, setting up meetings between those who demanded True Justice and those who insisted on rejecting it.

Moments before Aux-Ceras came into being, a perfect copy of Ceras' consciousness emerged from the DeepString pathways to be compiled and mapped onto a mass of polyform gel in a matter synth tube. Guided by an additional packet of biomorphic data, it took shape and, for all intents and purposes, became the same person as the Ceras back at the Council's Precinct deep within the Shroud. Of course, there were compromises. Polyform gel could only emulate biology, and didn't hold up to close medical scrutiny. But since this was far from a first contact situation, the Council agreed that it would have a negligible effect on his mission.

After Ceras' new window into the universe woke up, it was entangled through the DeepString with his Primary. It's not that they could connect or communicate. Rather, it ensured that if calamity were to arise, this twin consciousness would be pulled across the veil that suffuses the galaxy, the Span, and like a neuron firing from one edge of a grand brain to a specific point far and away – far and away – with experiences and information intact, back to the original mind.

The alternative was multiplicity. Although certain civilizations had no qualms about permanently duplicating a human consciousness, the Continuous Realms believed that however rare the process was, and however far afield a copy might go, this so-called anabranch must return in time or risk violating the sanctity of the self.

But in the meantime, this new Ceras was lying to the universe, and It didn't take kindly to those who messed around with Its established regulations, parameters, and realities – especially those who thumbed their noses at the speed of light so brazenly. Universal relativistic forces, the silent wardens of the space between stars and atoms alike, would be after him regardless of the Bank's efforts to pay the debt using some other reference point. But they would leave him alone if his sins against causality were resolved quickly...

Otherwise: what does it look like when the universe tries to balance the equation itself? Present-day citizens of the Continuous Realms needed only look to the Eastern Arm of the galaxy to see what could happen to those who exploited phenomena they barely understood.

Ceras had to be fast or his rejection of universal law would be expunged, which meant him, of course, along with anything or anyone in the vicinity during the 'correction'.

Luckily, that sort of thing didn't happen often. There would be signs as the bill came due.

But not much time to rectify the situation before:

Boom!

That's why the Bank was founded, after all: to account for humanity messing around with forces that they had some but not complete control over.

If a spontaneous and unmediated equalization event destroyed Aux-Ceras, the consequences for his Primary would be grave.

Being removed from reality, according to those who have watched it happen, does not look particularly painless.

People tend to scream.

So there you have it: Ceras had to resolve the conflict quickly or risk the wrath of the universe.

There were less egocentric reasons to get it resolved quickly, too. No one wanted to deal with another Long War, or to worry about the consequences of forbidden breakthroughs in FTL technology. But even so, it seemed likely that such technologies had been developed, and as unified as the Realms claimed to be, it was likewise possible that some of the further colonies had imagined a world beyond the Council's reach. If the secrets of the Span couldn't be controlled, diplomats like Ceras could at least try to keep fingers, talons, and pseudopods off the big red button.

Ceras had considered plenty of this in his lifetime.

Aux-Ceras massaged his recently formed throat and stretched out his muscles before settling into the captain's chair...

= WE HAVE ARRIVED, Ceras. =

The onboard intelligence that had calculated the last leg of his voyage had been given a deep and masculine voice. Unlike the one that had sent him here, which had been downright seductive.

Yet both had acted with perfect precision. The ship he had just appeared on had nearly arrived.

Umber, the Sunless World. It wasn't the only of its kind, so far as the Continuous Realms understood it. Indeed, many travelers had chosen to explore the uncharted frontiers the universe from the surface of free-floating worlds like Umber. Some of these so-called rogue planets had long ago lost their host star, while others were deliberately untethered by intrepid adventurers seeking the freedom that only the space beyond the Span could offer.

Yet unlike many of the civilizations within the Span that had openly defied the will of the Council, Umber had kept the exact nature of its sedition secret – and Continuous Laws applied only to objective reality, not rumor and innuendo.

Aux-Ceras needed to discover the truth.

After some silent negotiations between his ship and Umber's orbital network concluded, a direct line opened to his host, Deridan Maxwell, Master of Umber. "Welcome to our world, Arbiter Ceras. We appreciate that you have taken the time to join us and that the True Justice recognizes the importance of dialogue between our two worlds. I welcome you follow our escort wing to the landing area in the capital. It should join you shortly."

"I am humbled to be here, Host and Master; I am sure that your home will be a welcome change from the political theatre of the Continuous Realms. I hope we can find a quick and mutually beneficial resolution to our dispute."

"Likewise. Yet, we shall also see. May I ask you a favor before you complete the landing protocols?"

"Please."

"I am familiar with the Crusade starship class, Arbiter Ceras, and would ask that you power down the ship's core prior to entering our gravitational field. It is, as you might understand, in both our interests that there be trust built prior to your arrival. We have no reason to believe your word, nor have we any reason to acknowledge the authority of the

Continuous Realms, if there isn't some transparency on your side."

Not many still understood the principles underlying the millennia-old Crusade, and this surprise turn could make his mission more difficult. Nevertheless, Aux-Ceras was quite prepared to change his tactics; he wouldn't have been much of a negotiator otherwise.

"Of course, Host and Master. This will be done."

While he waited for the escort to arrive, Ceras made a tour of the old Crusade ship. It had long ago traveled the length that he had cheated, towing behind it the Span, the synthetic quantum web that lesser civilizations called a corruption of spacetime, but all acknowledged as one of the galaxy's great wonders. It was but one of countless more that had spread across the galaxy as fast as conventional engines allowed.

It was their fate to travel on their paths forever and ever. But after the Long War, all such ships were stopped in place – to be used only to facilitate border negotiations, but never again to emit the energy to spread the Span further.

The ship had spent its adolescence here, nestled in a Lagrange point around a distant, foreign star. It would be easy to believe that a hundred thousand years had lapped at its heels. And yet it waited. At the edge of the Continuous Realms, awaiting orders from those who might call upon it one day.

If you had a sense of the compromises a self-aware ship needed to make over the millennia to maintain itself, you would have likely said that it looked its age. Ceras had been just a boy when the last fleet of Crusade ships were sent off on their journeys, in a time before the twilight of the Long War. Before the survivors witnessed the signing and establishment of True Law, the abolition of Span expansion, and the Council's 500-year moratorium on DeepString development and use.

Oh, if only you had been there, friends, and witnessed the Collapse – the annihilation of the Eastern Arm of the Way Galaxy (what only the most hidebound historians call the Milky Way) – you would understand why the price for using the technology was so high.

You would understand why it inspired such fear. And why such sacrifices were made to control it.

The screams of those in the Shatter, that vast, impossible grave, would, if they could, travel the space between stars.

It was not always used for such evil, of course. Most of Ceras' family had been in DeepString transit when that happened, cruising out to the Eastern Frontier where the Realms had yet to make its presence known.

A place without war. A place free from their terrible ambition and their "True Justice". They are remembered only as victims of the Shatter now. And in the uncounted centuries since, he had forgotten the look of their faces and the sound of their voices. But not the pain of their loss. That has, like a scar, marked him for all of time.

He had been lucky, in contrast, to have been drafted to work in gestalt form with the other experts whose minds the Continuous believed would serve in unravelling the Last Great Mystery.

Now, so long after the end of the Long War, the answer still remains out of reach.

By any reasonable standard, the Crusade ship had long since exceeded its allotted lifespan. That it still functioned at all was a testament to the onboard intelligence's talent for self-preservation, which it had honed to a razor's edge over the centuries. If raw elements could talk, Ceras might have had some very enlightening conversations. But they remained silent, and the ship volunteered little about its past.

Yet a being is more than the sum of its parts, and through years of need and plenty, the Central Intelligence had matured – if not decayed – into something altogether different. Its sinister-sounding vocal circuits only told a fraction of the tale.

"Ship." Aux-Ceras stretched out, satisfied that they wouldn't find anything out of the ordinary there. "I would like you to recognize Code Hot Steam and behave appropriately when you are being interrogated. Nothing about the Realms, the Council, or my orders are to be divulged to Umberite authorities without explicit indication that they are already aware of them. Confirm."

= CONFIRMED, Ceras. =

"Good. Now, give me some Uplift so I can be at my best." It didn't respond; instead, a soft mist followed from the ports on the sides of the hallway. The moment they touched his biomimetic skin he felt invigorated, mind and body, and it was good timing.

"Arbiter Ceras." The voice seemed to come from the transmission centre of his neuro-implant. Even though the ship's matter synth hadn't been activated in centuries, this frame's resemblance to his actual body was truly uncanny. "We are here to guide you to the Capital. My name is Ulgrick, and my co-pilot is Temme. We are pleased to serve as your security detail, and hope that you find your stay with us a comfortable one. I have been assured you are prepared to power down when indicated. Shall we go?"

He returned the message with a mere thought. "Yes. Thank you, Ulgrick and Temme. Let's get going."

The escort craft, nearly as big as the Crusade ship, darted towards the gravity well of the rogue planet. It was barren, for the most part, but that information had been available in the preliminary report. There were small spots of civilization here and there, encased under enormous domes – albeit small relative to the planet itself.

One dome could easily have been the size of Australia back on Old Earth, another, the size of Europe, but they were relatively small, and that's how the Realms measured things.

In terms of land mass, population, and military might, they were a pebble in the sky when compared to the Realms, and even to the Autarchy that Umber was scheduled to meet. Like Earth would appear next to the red supergiant Betelgeuse.

They drew closer to the amplified magnetosphere and, as he was instructed, Arbiter Ceras shut off the power to the ship. His vacsuit generator came to life, forming a soft shell around his flesh, encasing him in a preservative field that could sustain him in environments that would vaporize even the near-immortal inhabitants of the Realms. It was a standard feature for Arbiters and those living outside Green Zones.

The technology was old, but effective.

= DON'T FORGET YOUR ORDERS, Ceras. =

The Ship sent a final, slurred reminder before falling into hibernation.

Meanwhile, and as the vacsuit finished forming, the ship found itself effortlessly attached to the guide belt from the lead escort. Ceras was quick to switch his perceptual feed to explore the view and data from the ship's perspective; even with the core deactivated, the passive sensors could continue to supply telemetry for hours.

It was all wrong, of course, but he didn't know it then. He sighed a little, feeling refreshed by what the data said. It should have bothered him. It was a hint, wasn't it?

Everything looked normal.

***

"Welcome to our world!" Host and Master Derridan Max- well reached out and shook his hands, one after the other. "I am so pleased to see that we have such a high ranking agent of the

Council joining us for this," he leaned in, "frankly absurd impediment on our rights as an independent state."

"I'm sure we'll be able to resolve all of this quickly enough."

"Yes, yes! Good saying, my friend!" The Host and Master was gregarious and warm, as opposed to the antagonistic prick that he had been made out to be by the Realms media.

"Where shall we start?" Ceras asked with a smile, knowing that Derridan had already felt enough direct pressure from the Council. "I think we should start with a taste of the culture here. I'll be handing you off to Temme, who will take you to our garden, and then to the Capital near the edge of our agricultural plots. He will want to record your conversations for review later, of course."

"Of course."

"Then, let's say around the midday feast, we'll meet with the elected officials here in preparation for the Autarchy's delegation." The Host and Master went to leave when Ceras added: "When do you expect Umber to enter orbit?"

He stopped. "Days, perhaps a week at most. Our gravitists have had some difficulty bending the warp of our shell to match the unique quality of the system's background energies."

"Yes, about that, the Realms are very interested in how–"

"All to be explored and perhaps even explained at a different time, Arbiter Ceras. Now, if you'll please excuse me, I have much to prepare for."

He left quickly, leaving Ceras with Temme, a small man with big, round, and eerily black eyes and a bald, shaved scalp. His teeth were golden and his skin tone, something like a light, transparent chrome set atop a pinkish base.

Ceras made a sharp contrast, matching a rich, dark tone with bright, chilling blue eyes, and stood at least a foot taller than his new companion.

"Fine to meet you, Arbiter."

"And you." Temme clapped his hands together, "Well, let's get going, shall we? Lots to see, lots to do, and people to meet! My, oh my, many people to meet."

"Reliable information on Umber is tough to come by in the news feeds or the Continuous Archives. How much, I wonder, are you allowed to discuss with me?"

"As long as it doesn't violate our sovereign right to privacy, I can pretty much tell you about anything. Father really wants you to be comfortable and for the people of the Continuous Realms to understand that while we're open to negotiation, we aren't going to be bullied."

"Father? The Host and Master is your father?"

"Apologies, I thought you were aware of that. Yes, all leading officials are directly related to the Maxwell genegroup. It ensures that we can properly serve the people without internal struggles or protests."

"Interesting... Rather like Old Earth prior to the abolition of the royal systems."

The man's black eyes widened, and Ceras thought he saw a translucent membrane slide across both.

"Old Earth?" He clapped again, this time with noticeable excitement. "Do you really have experience with people from the home- world?"

"I was born there." His grin swallowed itself into a grimace. "Certainly not! That would make you..." He counted, stopped, stared off into the distance, and came back with: "Old. Very, very old. Impossibly old. Unpleasantly old, perhaps."

"I'll be happy to provide you with details. I guarantee you that I am what I say I am."

Temme's head shook. "Let's forget that, for now at least. Come, come, we must get onto the Vein and travel to the Capital! You'll get a chance to see some of the cleverness of the Umberite people. We have done some wonderful things with superconducting lattices, to say nothing of the exotic materials we retrieved from the Sp–" He paused. "When we were experimenting with the technology that keeps Umber safely insulated from the interstellar medium."

The two walked through into a carrier car on a track and sat down. Since Ceras arrived, aside from the Host and Temme, there had been no sign that any other humans lived on the planet at all – even here, at a transit station, they were alone.

"Temme, tell me, why are you here?" His expression twitched. "Indeed, that's a good question. Why are we here? What is our purpose? Can we be sure there is such a thing?"

"I mea–"

"Yes, yes, I know what you meant. I'll have to defer to my father to give you a better explanation than I can. We have been traveling a long time, Arbiter. A very, very long time. We have seen such things that would haunt your mind, waking or asleep, until the day you chose to end it all. We have found ourselves face to face with phenomena and possibilities that would make the True Justice himself take leave of his senses and abandon millions of years of evolution in favour of the mindlessness of beasts. Yet, out there, in the great divide where so few are prepared to travel, we have come to the conclusion that, perhaps, together is better than alone."

Temme went to barely a whisper, "Without ears, it listens. Without a heart, it feels."

"What does?"

"The universe. Reality. Whatever you choose to call it." The car accelerated silently. Out they went, from the window-less station onto the surface of Umber. The cold, colourless terrain was almost smooth except for some rolling valleys and hills in the distance. Far off, beyond the shimmer of the gravity field, the Autarchy's brilliant blue star – as rogue as the planets that orbited it – was faintly visible.

Soon their representatives would arrive, and the Umberites' presentation would begin.

For now, there was something unattainably beautiful about the blue light twinkling just out of reach. Yet, its size grew with each passing moment.

"Loneliness doesn't seem much like the appropriate emotion to incite a war with the Continuous Realms, my young friend."

"We don't war, Arbiter. But, and I mean this by no way as a threat – rather, as a cautious statement that requires your attention, if I may usurp your polite language for the sake of brevity – If there were to be a war as a result of our overtures towards the Autarchy, and if convincing you is our battlefield, you should know that we will win it."

They rode on for a time accompanied by much more vague conversation regarding far less interesting things until, finally, the car rose up a hill and slowed as it settled into a large, artificial crater with a dome that shook as it was pierced and sealed behind them.

"Gods be good," Ceras gasped, nearly pressing his face to the window. "What beauty is this?" ***

Spurred on by the fading intelligence at its core, the Crusade ship's reserve energy flowed into the matter synth chamber. It wasn't enough that most security systems would take notice – or that was the hope, at least. From within the polyform gel, something like a human formed.

Umber had just passed into the Span, the energy field created long before its idealistic founders set a course into the abyss. This had, in turn, triggered the next phase in the Council's plan.

In moments, the Nemesis would be complete, and it would start about its task.

***

"I'm still absolutely dumbfounded by what you have done here, Temme." Ceras was gushing, and it was genuine. He kept looking out the window as the car made the circuit around the Capital. The crater was green and bright and beautiful.

"We extrapolated the information from our own genetic code." Ceras nodded, obviously confused. "We reverse engineered our genome as far back as we could, interpolating data where we had to, watching it branch out, trimming things here and there, and using new data to move even further back. Again and again for thousands of years. At first, we only tampered with samples from our archives, but eventually, we had a breakthrough and took leaps into prehistory. To a time when the Tree of Life was much more extensive, to a time when so many wonderful and impossible things emerged from the crucible of ancient Earth. This is the fruit of that labour of love, Arbiter Ceras – our secret, and our gift."

Out there, just beyond the morning fog, was a forest unlike any the universe had known for a quarter million years. It was lush, vibrant, idyllic, and any other word that could be used to describe something impossible to imagine in an era where, for the most part, humans weren't even human in form or function anymore.

Ceras, the real Ceras, certainly wasn't. To him, this seemed improbable and yet to others, he knew, it would seem wasteful.

What need did the universe or the Realms have for these things? One by one, the greatest minds in the galaxy had pushed humanity far beyond the petty limitations of organic existence.

"I think"– Ceras hesitated for an agonizing moment – "I think you may have a case."

"We know we have a case, Arbiter Ceras, and we expect our petition to join the Autarchy – even as it technically lies within your territory – will proceed without incident. But by virtue that you also see it this way, perhaps there will be peace in our time after all. We do not want wish to revisit the Long War, do we?"

Still entranced, Ceras could only nod in agreement.

The car slowed as it turned into a spiral that ran into a grass-layered tunnel near one side of the forest. It was disappointing that the view was gone but there would, he hoped, be time to explore the wonders the Umberites had created.

"Now that we'll be heading into the Capital, this is going to come as a bit of a shock, so I'm going to have to ask you to refrain from asking the obvious questions about our technology. Is that acceptable?"

"I suppose. There will be an opportunity to see more of that wonderful place, won't there?" Ceras shifted back and forth in anticipation. "I never thought I'd see another tree, not a real one like that, anyway."

"There might be time, but that is only a small portion of what we have done. Arbiter, come, stand here." Temme urged him to the other side of the car and, moments later, they exited from the tunnel.

"Gods be good, indeed..."

***

The Nemesis had doubled itself in the last ten minutes, which brought its number to sixteen – each one going about in perfect unison, removing panels from the walls, floors, ceilings, and everywhere else they could and refitting them into something else.

***

Umber, Ceras now understood, was not so difficult to move after all. The core of the planet had been hollowed out, leaving the crust as a shell for what stood within. And what a marvel it was. Umber's entire inner surface was green with patches of blues and other natural colours. Sitting at its core, a half-bright, half-dark sphere was rotating on an enormous axle that ran from the top to the bottom. In the shadowy areas at the poles, domed cities crawled up towards the pivoting beam. It was no wonder that the Umberites insisted he deactivate his core, considering the incredible gravitational engineering required to support single-gee settlements on both sides of the crust.

Even from here, Ceras could see the colossal walls that separate areas of different colours and consistencies from one another. Great jungles, towering dunes, frozen tundras – words that had long since lost all but the vaguest literary significance were here, given life and form in a world that the True Justice's star-spanning intellect could never have imagined. Ceras wept for a home that could only dream of secrets that killed.

"Paradise..." Ceras sighed, enveloped in the unreal

warmth of an impossible star, confronted by such beauty that he felt himself fall his knees.

"We have been at this for a very long time, Arbiter, but we feel it is time that we brought this back to our people. First the exiles, the travellers in dark places, those who refused the urge to control. And someday, once the wandering worlds of the Autarchy bring the borderlands into bloom, perhaps even the Realms themselves. We will not keep secrets from you, but neither will we hasten to show the Council the way. Yet our doors will always be open to the peaceful.

These creatures are natural, pure, untampered – save for the boundaries separating each ecosystem – and they reach back so far that they have revealed more about what and who we are than anyone had ever suspected. We have come here for you, our brethren, but even this is not the greatest gift that we offer. But my father will tell of that."

"H-How... W–...This is... I can't..."

"We will arrive at the Capital soon, there, you will learn more. For now, enjoy the journey as we have marveled in its creation and its many rewards."

***

The doubling had stopped at one hundred and ninety-six. The many-bodied Nemesis was a singular mind that knew precisely what needed to be done and worked tirelessly towards that end. Some humanoid forms had sacrificed their polyform flesh to become components of the Great Work, diminishing in number but increasing in speed.

They would be finished soon.

***

"Father, I have taken our guest on a tour of our home." Temme bowed and stepped back, ushering Ceras to a seat next to the Host and Master. He sat down, still shaken by what he had witnessed but holding himself together.

"And what does the Arbiter have to say for himself?" Host and Master Maxwell gave Ceras a warm hug, making him feel like he'd returned home. "Quite the sight, isn't it?"

"I am humbled by your home, Host and Master."

"Now that you have seen what we have to offer, please refer to me as Derridan." He smiled, golden teeth shining like all the others sitting at the rounded table.

"Derridan," Ceras said, letting his voice carry through the assembly chamber, "it is my finding that the suspicions against you and your world are groundless. I am prepared to take word back to the Continuous Realms and the True Justice to see that any further action is suspended and that your rights as an independent state are upheld."

Applause and cheers carried through the chamber. "That is great to hear! We are glad that –" Derridan's head cocked to the right. His eyes darted back and forth. His jovial expression vanished and his black eyes turned white.

"WHAT IS THE MEANING OF THIS?" he shouted. The Master grabbed Ceras by his collar and threw him to the tabletop, knocking off empty plates and pans. "WHAT IS THE MEANING OF YOUR LYING WORDS?"

Ceras, stunned, said nothing. "I am told that there are creatures building something out of that Crusade ship of yours. What are they doing? Tell me now and we may yet resolve this peacefully."

The Nemesis? But that had always been a weapon of last resort... Ceras thought.

"I... I... You need to stop them from completing the structure! You have to destroy it! You can't let it be completed – if you don't, then –"

***

The DeepString snapped and in flurry of pain and confusion, memories of the betrayed Parallel swung across the vast expanse of broken space, far and away... far and away.

***

But the dying gasps of Umber left an indelible mark on the Span's geometry. Days folded into decades which turned themselves to millennia and then, at last, Aux-Ceras returned to its point of origin.

This hero, the man that had extinguished the fires of rebellion before they could spread into the Realms, was enjoying a cup of tea in his estate. Legions of admirers – followers, even –still made the pilgrimage well into the era of the Evening Empire, where the Council and the True Justice reigned no more. Those who tended to him, praised him, and adored him for who he was and what he did, believed his Auxiliary had simply shattered in the explosion of Umber in a heroic effort to save the Continuous Realms from another Long War.

As the source of its instincts, intellect, and loyalty to the Realms, Ceras-Prime had been rewarded in its stead.

By all accounts, the return of his Auxiliary after so many thousands of years should have shattered Ceras' mind and body, and transformed the bulk of his home planet into pure energy.

But this time, the universe took no payment. It only watched. His tears were not enough to stave off the deafening screams that heralded Umber's destruction.

His rage was not enough to absolve himself of the atrocity that he had been a part of. Even the release of death would be poor recompense for the wonders he had seen, and destroyed, on that peaceful, tranquil world.

The Master of Umber once promised him that if there was a war to be fought that they would win.

He was right.

THE FALL

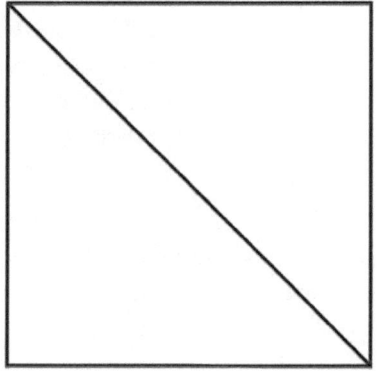

A GIRL & HER GOLEM

"It's this way?" the woman asked, placing a hand on her chin and looking at the terrain ahead. "I mean – you're sure this is it?" She turned around, sending golden hair twisting over her shoulder. She wore a strange, form-fitting dress, also gold, that stood out in stark contrast with her dark skin and deep-blue eyes.

A steam whistle suddenly emerged from her companion's right shoulder, joyously announcing their arrival to anyone within a good half-mile.

"What was that?"

"I do not know." The man... the thing standing next to her was more metal than man these days. His body was a mangled melange of meat and machinery encased in poorly polished chrome plating, each contour marked by the dimples and dents of a thousand battles. Each implant might have told its own tale, from his steel-hooved feet to the trumpets that listened where ears might once have been. One eye, the left, was hidden behind a thin black cloth. Mirdova had been traveling with her companion for long enough to have taken the time to assess – or diagnose – what she believed to be the order in which he had been 'upgraded'.

"I'm sure this is the way." The whistling stopped and

the noisemaker retreated to its hiding place below his right shoulder. "If we're going to sneak into the compound, you're going to have to shut that thing off." She took the first step up a steep climb that edged the side of the Weathered Mountains.

"What if it's keeping me alive?" He followed her, his colossal frame making less noise than before, but still enough to give a decent bearing to anyone who had heard the steam whistle.

"Can't we switch over to you 'brute-strength' personality for a while? When you get all mopey I feel like I'm going to be sick."

"It wouldn't really help. If I don't have someone to target, I might shut down again."

She considered this for a time, moving up with some difficulty. Her leg was still pretty banged-up from the fall back in the Way- march. The Creature, called such because he has no memory of his name, had saved her more than a few times in their years together. He'd done so without any demands or desires.

He owed her, sure. Mirdova had been the one that had worked out the combination to his cold coffin.

"We wouldn't want that." She was a little sarcastic, but that slight paranoia was new. New like the Creature's incipient personality. Sure, he had a temperament of sorts before... but ever since they entered the Waymarch, his determination was focused to a point. He knew where he had to be, even if he wasn't certain what was waiting for them there. The cold coffin she'd discovered in the junklands was old by anyone's standards. Hundreds, thousands, perhaps even tens of thousands of years of debris concealed it below the layers of garbage and old-world waste. He was no help in discovering anything more about his origins, either.

They'd had fun, though. She smiled. "Say, Creat, you remember Dolataria?" He turned around and revealed his face, one of only a handful (yes, one of his hands too) of things that were still part of his old self. There had been some freezer-burn and when they first met his nose had to be removed in the Triste Slumward near where he had been unearthed.

"I do." He nodded. "Do... Do you think we can do that again?"

"I have never denied you before." He reached for her. It was the right hand that brushed against her arm first. It was cold. Unpleasantly so. Then, the other reached down and up she went, left to rest on his shoulders.

"You're sure this doesn't bother you?" she asked, knowing the answer.

"No."

"And that... uh... whistle-thing – it won't pop up and throw me off your back, will it?" She felt him shrug. "That's comforting. You tell me if anything feels off and I'll jump down, 'kay?"

"Sure." He didn't always sound so colloquial. When they first met, Creature had been nearly mute. He understood things but he had difficulty finding his own words. He could obey back then. He wanted to obey back then... She shook off that memory. "Dolataria was beautiful." Creature said. "I really enjoyed living there. Do you ever... wish we had taken up the Commandant's offer? He was quite taken by you. You could have had some kids and – oumf!" She gave him a kick in his muscled left side.

"Shut up already." They were making much better time with Creature setting the pace. His legs rarely tired – though they did need to be oiled periodically. But the Weathered Mountains presented the type of terrain that you were meant to shake your fist at, much less actually take on seriously. All the same, up they went, following a worn footpath that slithered on the edge of life and the Mortual Chasm that ran the length of the mountain chain.

"The world's zipper," she thought out loud. "It was formed by the Ruu-shans in the Yolde Days." Sometimes Creature knew things. But he didn't know that he knew them. They just... flowed out when opportunities presented themselves. It was infuriating if you wanted specifics, but wonderful if you were prepared to be surprised by occasionally useful information.

"What happened?" Mirdova asked, leaning forward. She was dwarfed by her companion in the way a child might appear when standing next to a sizeable adult.

"There was a war. There is always a war. The enemy was advancing and the Ruu-shan Tzar refused to let his people fall to the hands of the Barb Ariens. He utilized the geoforming tech they used to attract deep water and thermal chutes for their power plants as a weapon." His voice changed, taking on an unfamiliar accent. "'It was as though the Earth itself was water. Flowing beneath our feet. I turned to my garrison and gasped as the seams in the concrete tore free and a gaping maw ripped wide open like a hungry jaw. As innumerable members of both armies fell into the abyss, others, like myself, were lifted into the sky on pillars the Tzar could not command. When I awoke, the ground was a touch warm and spouts of boiling water were soaking those who remained as the frigid temperature bit at our exposed flesh. I didn't need to hear from the Union. We had lost against the power of Nature herself.' That was the account of a soldier marching on the Ruu-shan capital."

"Is that where we're going, Creat?"

"I'm not sure. I think so. It could be something else." The Ruu-shans hadn't been a major power in the Sifican Reach for at least two thousand years. They certainly hadn't had geoforming technology when, history books say, they were finally overrun by the True Barbs. Their cities were devastated. Their numbers, literally decimated.

One in ten were taken from their major cities and slaughtered for every day the Last Tzar refused to surrender. Finally, after six days, the True Barbs' leader, Zhin Kahn, turned to the people of the walled Ruu-shan capital and promised that they would be left alone if they brought him the head of their beloved leader. It's not hard to imagine what they did. After the Tzar's personal guard fell defending him, the politicians that remained began to literally kill each other over the implied privilege of being the one to bring the old man's head to their conquerors.

The offer was, of course, a lie. If they had taken the time to peer over the battlements, they might have seen the True Barbs ready to storm the fortress as soon as the gates opened, no matter who beheaded whom. But as generations have said since then, promises are the true casualties of war.

Mirdova might not have grown up in a golden age of civilization, but some stories just carry forward. Some stories cannot be killed. She had heard the stories of the Ruu-shans, but despite the tales of their staggering powers, time smoothed out their impact on history like sand over a statue. Next to the empire-shattering power of Magnus Sterling's Aether Troops, simple geoforming weaponry seems almost laughable.

"How old are you?" she asked. "You have asked that every day for... almost ten years, Mirdova. I still don't have an answer for you. I promise – you'll be the second to know."

She'd hoped that the memory he'd just reclaimed would offer additional personal information like it did when they were in Dolataria. But, again, that was her hope talking. Her instincts, as always, told her that this story – as vivid as it had been – was no more relevant than the hundreds of other snapshots he had recalled over the years.

"Get some rest," he said to her, and while she fought her fatigue, Mirdova found herself ill-equipped to win – and after a few minutes of quiet she succumbed. Creature continued his walk, at a slightly reduced speed to keep her comfortable as she drifted into a deep dreamstate.

"Do you know what they're doing to him?" Mirdova screamed at her father. "He's probably in pain! I can't believe you care so little about that poor man!" She was fourteen. She'd never been further out than the Seven Slumwards and the Junklands beyond.

He'd used their discovery of the cold coffin as leverage. He wanted out of the scrap heaps and the blistering heat. At first, it wasn't about handing it over to the right people or the wrong people. It was about getting it working so that it could help them. But at their local technomancer's garage, the old man learned that this freakish creation could fetch a pretty sum, and went to the one group of people who had the means to pay it. Sadly, that kind of wealth didn't come from dealing fairly with every two-bit scrapmonger who walked through their gates.

She was tired and it had only been a few hours since her father, Merdoza, had sold the cold coffin's contents to the Minor-Tzar, Emrick. He had offered to throw in the coffin itself as a show of good faith, but Emrick had already sent his men to haul it away.

She woke to shouting and found him already three bottles deep into the Nebre Slumward's cheapest hooch.

"Get the hell out of here, you little bitch!" He took a swing at her. "As useful as your deadbeat brother and whore mother." He wasn't being figurative or colourful in his language. Her brother, Merk, had been beaten to death by Emrick's men when he was caught stealing food a few years ago. Her mother, well, she made do any way she could. Mirdova loved her father despite all of this. He'd raised her. He had kept their hopes high and their lives meaningful for so long, but now, he had finally succumbed to their desperate situation and fallen into the depths of despair.

Her father would sober up. He'd apologize. Everything would return to the way it was before. Not great, sure, but they had each other...

Only... That's not how things happened. Time went on by. Legends of the Steel Golem grew. He was described as a brute. A strong-armed demon. He was unstoppable – and so was Emrick.

Her father, on the other hand, found his reward for the man in the cold coffin to be sizeable enough that he never needed to stay sober again. And he had no intention of doing so.

So he continued to drink, and his anger exploded into violence. Mirdova could no longer see the kindness hiding under the mask of inebriation. She wondered Where did you go? but knew that she could not find him without eliminating his means of self-destruction.

One day while he was out she, went about the task of pouring out all his liquor until none remained. It took hours, and enough liquid had met the ground that it was soggy and mud-like. Its acrid odour lingered in the air and burned her eyes, ready to ignite the neighbourhood at the slightest spark.

When her still-drunk father discovered this, he naturally threw a fit. Merdoza dragged her out of their home and made a brisk walk towards the gates of the Minor-Tzar's compound. Outside, he screamed and begged the guards for just one more bottle. He pleaded so pitifully, some who watched told Mirdova afterwards, that they saw a guard throw a bottle from the parapets down to him.

Mirdova left, content with a new job out in the Near Junklands and pleased at the prospect of returning to a man that resembled her father, if only a little worse for wear from withdrawal. She looked forward to it, even. So it came to pass that on a cloudy midmorning, Mirdova returned from an early scrap-haul to find the Slumward's chief physician in their hut, smelling the bottle her father had drunk so gleefully. Shaking his head with regret. Asking if she'd had any, too. He had died just hours after their parting and, falling backwards into the muddy soil, had been swallowed up to his face.

There are vermin in the slums. Need any more be said? Later that same day, Mirdova found herself standing in front of the gates to Emrick's walled estate, screaming at whomever was willing to lend an ear.

"You killed my father, you – you bastards!" By dusk she was behind the bars of a grimy basement cell, awaiting some awful fate. Probably in the Minor-Tzar's harem, possibly at the end of a rope in the courtyard. Neither were futures that she would welcome.

Only... That's not how things happened. The Creature, despite their time apart, recognized her from when he first awoke from his long sleep. He was quiet and seated in the cell across from her, as he always was when Emrick had no need for him. They started to speak and both sides, over the course of many hours, came to a realization. Their fates were being controlled by the same terrible man. So then and there, Mirdova and the Creature made a pact.

They would leave the estate and find a place where they were welcomed and life was good. They weren't going to settle for less than paradise. They had had enough of the hell they were in now – Mirdova for what the place had done to her family, and the Creature for his stolen memories and brutal master. She promised there would be no more needless deaths. That she would take care of him.

At dawn, fires at their back, the two walked out of the estate as they would for years to come – Mirdova asleep in the arms of a metal avenger. The Minor-Tzar was dead, his men scattered to the winds.

There was little doubt that the Creature was a force to be reckoned with – and more importantly, that despite his appearance and dull-eyed deference to authority, he was human after all.

***

"It's time to get up, Dova," he said to her, and she yawningly obeyed, wiping the sleep from her eyes, feeling the coolness of the altitude gust through the blanket from their travel bag.

"Wh–" She stopped. "What did you call me?"

"Do you like it? I just thought it would be nice to try something new." He smiled.

"What's going on?" She stepped up and as she rose, so did the contours of the ruins of a huge city surrounded by mountains. "An... Acropolis?"

"Actually, we used to call these things metropolises. I lived here for a while, long ago." He stood next to her, feeling a throbbing in his head. "I don't know what's happening. But the memories are flooding back in. See that over there?" He pointed to a crippled skyscraper. "I used to work there. I had an office on the twenty-fifth storey and a laboratory that I ran in the sub-basement floor 10." Mirdova looked at him, momentarily saddened. Every time he remembered something about his past he said the same thing. It never stayed. At least, not all of it.

"You were a technomancer?" She laughed, pretending for both their sakes that she hadn't heard threads of the same story when they were in other strange locales. "I find that very unlikely."

"We didn't have technomancers back then, but I don't know what I was. Only... pieces of who I was. It's like an outline without substance or context. It feels... good, though. I feel like we're close to the paradise we've always wanted to find. If I'm wrong...

Well, I'd be okay if went back to Dolataria." He reached out and squeezed her hand with his real one. "I'm sorry about..."

"I know." She squeezed back and gave him a hug. "I don't really know if I like these new personality traits, though." She smirked. "I hope you can still kick some ass if we need you to."

He smiled back. "Don't you worry. Come on, there's a way down somewhere near here."

As they approached the edge, a dim surface flickered ahead of them.

"Stop!" She grabbed him. "That's a WarField. You'll be torn apart!" He turned to her around, let go of her hand, and stepped into the darkness.

Heart swelling and horror climbing up her spine, Mirdova watched him vanish. There was a pause. "Aren't you coming?" His disembodied voice was hard to hear. "Huh?" she said, overcome with honest surprise and something dangerously close to elation.

He stepped back and tugged her through the buzzing, tingling membrane.

"No. Way." The city ahead of them was still in ruins, but the field had obscured – and perhaps protected – something neither of them could have foreseen. It was huge. Taking up a clearing in the centre of the metropolis that was easily the size of the slumward she'd grown up in. It shined brightly against the dilapidated concrete.

"Can you fly that thing?"

"I... I know I can." He rubbed a patch of chrome on head. "The question is, where do we go?"

"Where can we go?"

"Theoretically? Anywhere. It will replenish its batteries the moment we start up the reactor and get it airborne."

"Anywhere?"

"Seems that way."

"You've brought us this far, Creat. Where do you think we should go next?"

He considered this for a moment. "It's called... Mezopo. It was built on the southern pole. Hidden away. That's where the others will be." He seemed so sure and yet so uncertain. It was in these silent moments that Mirdova found herself following the stretches of flesh along his body to where they blended into the metal shell. Occasionally, she'd notice the small openings where gears whirred and the buzz of electricity kept her companion moving. Kept him alive. He couldn't travel if it rained, though that wasn't much of a problem these days. It rained, what, two, perhaps three times a season? Hardly enough to keep the cisterns full. Water was like gold. It was life. Here stood a man whose Achilles heel was the very thing that women and men now fought to the death to claim for their own. Here stood a Creature that, far more than he was man or machine, was a living mystery.

How had his sleepless mind survived all these years? Why was he so driven to follow the feeling – and that's all it was, intuition carved from the walls of a dream – that there was something waiting for him out there, something better than the rusted kingdoms of a dying world that they'd slowly explored over a dirty decade?

He repeated again, questioning it: "That's where the others will be?"

"Others?"

"We used to call them survivors." He put a hand up. "I don't know why I said we, but isn't that exciting? Maybe there are others like me out there. Maybe they have a way to make me whole again."

She snorted. "Survivors? Kinda rude to call 'em that, isn't it? What are we if we aren't survivors? And what were these people surviving?" She spat. "The hell with them! We made it pretty far without whatever those fancy Mezopo people have."

There was that pause again. Gears and cogs, churning around in a mostly-bloodless shell. His noseless face scared others. His disjointed personality had been used against them more than once in their travels. But on days like this, when the man behind the steel mask and synthetic voice truly woke up... well, she liked that. She liked to whisper it to herself from time to time as they walked: 'He is human.'

"Where do you want to go?" he asked her. Already,

the scraps of memory that had so invigorated him when they walked through the barrier were fading, as though the dull machine mind was somehow stronger than his afterthought of a brain – for when the Man awakened, the Machine was never far behind.

"We'll find our paradise, won't we old friend?" He smiled, but less than before. "I'd rather not answer that." He reached out, thought better of it, and stared off into the distance.

"No. I take that back. We're definitely going to find it. Wherever it is. Whatever it is."

Mirdova regarded him with a wink and a tap on the back. He had regained so much since they first met. It didn't always come to the surface like it was now, but it was in there, somewhere.

"This is the right path to be on," Mirdova mouthed to herself, slowly giving it voice. "Because he is human. Because I am human." Not for the first time, she knew this was where she wanted to be: with him.

It was always exciting. It was sometimes frightening, but always tinged with intrigue and the unknown. It was everything that life back in the Slumwards could never be. This was the world. It was mostly empty for all they knew. It was incredibly lonely at times, soul-crushing in light of what things should have been.

But! She didn't miss having a place to call home

anymore. Wherever they went, somehow, became home.

And if they didn't find what they were looking for at this Mezopo pole-thing, well, they were always welcome back in Dolataria. It was fun there. It was beautiful. And, because of them, it was now a safe place to be. Mirdova gripped the sacred blade they had given her to commemorate the timely death of the Geo- phage. The two of them put down an overgrown worm, and they'd wanted to make her queen. Imagine that! Her? A queen. Pfft, it wasn't even a question worth entertaining.

Still... Even if she rejected the regency... She could live there and be pretty happy. Right? A few hundred people in one place, without thirst or hunger? She'd never get over the joyous absurdity of that thought.

The two wanderers walked down to the airship. It would need work before it would fly. Patches here and there. But they had time. They had all the time in the world.

***

The sun was bright. It was always bright, but today, it seemed a touch more.

A warm breeze swept over them and out and away. Far away. To places they would visit someday. It touched on people and stories that would bring the Creature, and Mirdova, closer to who they really were and wanted to be.

***

Time passed. With a push of a button the enormous craft took flight with the two sitting at the helm.

The Creature asked again, "Where to?" Mirdova gave him a hug and a light peck on the cheek. "Let's go find out!"

THE □□□

WHAT WERE WE EXPECTING?

"I just don't understand why
people talk about opening Pandora's
Box like it's a bad thing," Adeline
remarked to her sister, who was busy
reeling an old rope in the window with
a squeaky winch.

"Yeah, yeah. I know. Please,
can we not have this conversation
now?" She considered this and added: "Especially not right
now?"

"Well, like Nanna says, it's either now or never,
right?"

"It's just"– Laurel remembered where she was,
bringing her voice down to a conspiratorial whisper – "It's just
like you to make me do your homework the day it's due! Trust
me. I was the one who mentioned it."

"Were you?" Adeline scratched her head. "I could
swear..."

" Oh, come on! That first chat we had, I mentioned
that even with everything else they get wrong about Pandora's
Box, most people don't realize that it was actually a pithos."
She used her free hand to outline a shape while the other hand
labored to bring up the rest of the rope. " The idea that it's a
box is only a few hundred years old. Doesn't this ring a bell?"

"Right! That sounds... sorta familiar. Pithos..."
Adeline scrolled through her mind for an answer, immediately
relented, and reached for her iPhone for answers. "Ugh.
You're so useless sometimes. It's just a big jar." Laurel spun
around in the office chair, letting her hair loose from its clip
and transforming, momentarily, into a blurry hair-tornado.
"What- ever! It doesn't matter. We both agree. It's weird."

"Yeah," Adeline said. As the older of the two, she
didn't like to play the sidekick, but here she was.

"And it's also weird that the Greeks said the Bo – I'm
sorry, the Jar, was left filled with hope. 'Is something like
True Hope denied us for want of a pithos?'"

Adeline sighed, mouthing the rest of the words as
they had been written in the ledger. Memorization came easy
to her, as her grades and careful diction showed. Her capacity
for original thought was more difficult to gauge.

Laurel frowned at her sister's attempts to contribute,
but couldn't deny the quote from the ledger was germane to
their quest. "See, that wasn't so hard. Now put your phone
away and let's get a move on so we can find out if that's true
or not."

Laurel hopped off the chair and landed on her bare
feet. The muffled sounds of the struggling (albeit tightly
bound) security guard in the corner were starting to get on her
nerves. She looked at the screens, each cycling through a
series of static cameras monitoring the museum.

"Okay," Adeline said, giving her sister an encompassing hug, "but Mum and Dad are going to be so mad when they find out."

"Shhh." Laurel smiled. "They'll be glad. Come on, it's time." She picked up the old ledger from the counter. Its worn leather cover had bled away most of the stain, and the embossed gold leaf monogram had long since faded. It had once belonged to the man down the way, in the old house by the smelly creek.

He gave it to Laurel during one of her morning jogs. It was a new habit that she was developing for when she finally built up the courage to go out for the cross country team, and finally break into her sister's traditional athletic territory. Anything to bridge the year between them, and the social gulf that always felt wider. It was only a few days later that same week, on her normal morning jog, that she stopped and spotted the ambulance carrying out a black, human-shaped bag and realized that its significance had grown immeasurably.

Whatever secrets that handwritten book contained belonged to her now.

They hadn't been terribly close, the old man and her. Laurel wasn't really close to anyone, save for her sister. It was a product of being ahead of the curve, as her parents said. She was just too bright for her own good, and in their small town, not much could be done to accommodate her advanced intellect and thirst for knowledge.

It got her in trouble. Despite their differences, the

man had somehow helped her develop better coping mechanisms than resorting to what her mother despondently called Laurel's smarty-pants tantrums.

The man had been smart too. And kind. And he had listened to the questions that kept her awake, and responded with stories that saturated her active imagination with possibilities of what lay beyond the hills and trees – he had given her insight into the world, and for that she would be eternally grateful.

A friendship had budded, nurtured by those times he would wave her over as she was going by. He was often seated during these exchanges, body bent and twisted by time but smiling and rocking back and forth against the wind in his old chair. He affected a bow-tie and occasionally fiddled with the pipe otherwise perched on the corner of his weather-tested table beside a small pile of tobacco and cloves.

He wouldn't smoke when she was around, but not long after their customary meeting, she would smell the blended aroma following her down the path into the forest's edge.

It was the same every time: she would be running down the laneway, counting her steps and keeping a record of her time clocked away in her mind, and he would greet her with a gentle nod and offer tea and biscuits.

She rarely refused him. All in exchange for a few minutes spent listening to him chat about what and who he used to be – and it wasn't difficult either, because, for her, it was always fun to hear his stories. He'd go on about the Great

War and how charismatic the leaders had been back then.

Her parents knew him, and after her jogs would ask her about the old man.

Her father, a native to the town, had grown up and become so accustomed to seeing the man that he scarcely paid him any mind at all. Truthfully, that had become more difficult in the recent years, as the man took to sitting outside his home more frequently since his wife passed. Attempting, poorly, to strike up a conversation with each and every person that traveled along the path.

At first, it was interesting, but once you came to realize that the stories were always the same, and that he seldom if ever had any intention of reciprocating with a thoughtful ear in return, well, that route became less popular.

Laurel and Adeline's father wondered if the man knew this fact – that he had become a reason to detour around the block.

It was hard to imagine a mind, especially one so sharp and aware as his, that wouldn't have realized. It was sad, too, because there was a time the man was a paragon of health and sociability, respected by the community, even including her father. That said, her father was quick to admit that the man had always been degrees in favour of odd.

Her mother, a few years younger, was less critical. She'd babysat the old man's kids when she was just a teenager and found the family, well – yes, a little eccentric, but certainly not dangerous.

Adeline couldn't be bothered to form an opinion either way. At fifteen, she had far better things to do than talk about people with the gall to live offline, which made her consistent support for Laurel's adventure all the more puzzling. Laurel wondered if she just liked to practice sneaking out, but her presence made this easier... and more fun.

Now that the old man's brood had left town, both parents could appreciate that the man was a little lonely. In this they approved their daughter's interaction with him – so long as it was done outside his house. Not that they suspected ulterior motives or that his eccentricity had curdled into something dangerous, but... well, a parent hears things about neighbours on the news here and there, and a little caution never hurt anyone.

Only once had Laurel broken that promise. Three weeks ago, on the day that she received his ledger – the one that had led her here with her older sister in tow, into the dark, mould-mottled museum with its tall ceilings and ornate doorways – it hadn't been particularly cold. This seemed strange to Laurel as she considered the event in hindsight.

'Aren't grand adventures meant to start with some ominous force of nature?' She imagined the old man's weary skepticism about the proper accompaniment to a quest even as they crept down the stairs and out the backdoor of their Victorian-era home, stepping cautiously around the spots in the old flooring that they knew would creak and alert their parent-captors of their curfew-break- ing plans.

But then, only a few steps away, when they were sure they weren't going to be heard, there was a distant sound that she took for thunder, and that alone was enough to sharpen her eyes and quicken her heart in anticipation of the adventures to come.

All of this, begun from that ledger. Laurel's need to investigate manifested when she had reached about a third of the way through the convoluted collection of notes and academic writing, when her eyes fell on a particular page, festooned with pencil sketches repeatedly encircled with deep red ink and the words: "It's here! I can't believe I've finally found it! And they don't even know what they have... It has to be..."

The old man's (for who else's could it be?) joyous, frantic scribblings trailed off where the pages were faded by wear – and, if Laurel's suspicions were correct, by water.

After drafting Adeline into the investigation, the two excitable girls combed Wikipedia pages for Pandora's B... Jar, and came to the same (okay, maybe the investigation was heavily biased towards Laurel) conclusion of what had to be done.

After the portentous crackle of thunder, the two were forced to wander the grove separating the east and west sides of town to find the unlit back door of the museum. They'd done some reconnaissance the week before, and found it was left unlocked while the security guard was on duty.

Speaking of whom: Fidger Winks, the town drunk, and only acting security guard at the Gladewood Museum, had already passed out from his traditional ten-thirty gin. It made restraining him an easy enough task – and with her first field test, Adeline proved an able student of knot tying. Before settling down, Fidger surprised the pair a few times with muffled complaints and thrashing movements that were, in all likelihood, unrelated to being tied up and more due to a deteriorating frame and thinning airways.

He wasn't supposed to smoke inside the museum, but had realized long ago that its miasmic aroma and general muskiness was more than enough cover for his favorite cigarettes. By the time his would-be quarry had made their way from the back door to his small office, he'd already let one of his carcinogenic companions burn down to its filter. It was still in his hand, readying itself to bite at his fingers with embered fire. It wouldn't have made much of an impact, they noticed, displaying their best yuck faces at the other blisters, burns, and calluses on his hands and arms. It must have been a remarkably common occurrence – some force must be looking out for him if that was the case.

Laurel and Adeline were definitely good girls at heart (even if they were trespassing) and so, without a moment's hesitation, they removed the red-tipped saboteur before it could damage him any further.

Now, preparing to carry out the instructions in the book, the two were stretching and tracing their path on the map near the door. It was going to be a good sprint to the classics section on the other side of the small-town museum because in just a few minutes' time, the alarm was going to...

"You ready?" Laurel asked, and her sister nodded.

She pressed the manual reset for the alarm system. It wasn't as though it was hard to figure out. The sequence was spelled out right there with all the information carefully listed for even the most gin-soaked mind to comprehend. It meant they had minutes before it came back online to complete their task. Until that time, however, the security system was as disabled as Fidger himself.

This plan was deliberate and technical, and it had not been their own.

The old man had run through it a number of times. Pages that followed the sketches were filled with aged photographs captioned words that were lost when he died. It let the imagination of the young women wander, though. Had the old man with the laneway house been an Indiana Jones of sorts? Travelling the world and purchasing, retrieving, or otherwise collecting artefacts from places others were unable or unwilling to explore?

It didn't matter. They were the heroes now. Rushing out the door and tapping their soft shoes on the cold tile as they continued on towards their destination.

"Faster! FASTER!" Laurel whispered then shouted, hoping her sister would grace them with her legendary speed, knowing that they had so little time to complete their task.

They made their way through static snapshots of history – passing by preserved bog-mummies, death masks, old books, scrolls, and images of famous dig sites, each accompanied by a plaque that explained, at length, what each piece depicted and why they were significant. A reconstruction of a large prehistoric sloth stood above them, its cold eyes peering over the displays like a silent (and sleepy) guardian. Murals, some dating from Mesopotamian times, rested on shelves that were rotting at their bases. The Gladewood Museum's endowment, once the pride of the city, had seen better days – and if something weren't done soon, these treasures would soon collapse and shatter into dust.

At the entrance to the ancient Greek exhibit sat an exact replica of the Rosetta Stone. Next to it, hidden under a white sheet coated in dust, was the old man of the laneway's last discovery. A treasure that was but two feet in height placed so close to the edge of the entryway that it had been presumed to be a table by some ill- informed curator, intern, or volunteer. (Adeline thought it might have been Fidger, in a late-night display of decorative flair.) Atop the sand-worn cube, a few shiny cards were placed in a basket with the note: "PLEASE LEAVE YOUR TICKETS HERE SO THEY CAN BE REUSED."

As it turns out, it had been the curator, and one that had been very conscious of the global impact of paper waste, introducing laminated tickets that could be recycled internally. As it turns out, it had been the curator, and one that had been very conscious of the global impact of paper waste, introducing laminated tickets that could be recycled internally. Digital technology could have easily gone the extra step, but the curator had been quite proud of this practice and kept it until he retired the year before. Now, the museum's crew had diminished to but three: the drunkard, Fidger; the guide, Cassie; and the janitor, Michelle. The occasional graduate student supplemented the museum's staff, but the collection was so well-documented that few academics bothered to make the trip.

They ran by the replica of the Rosetta Stone without a second thought, and brushed just enough against the white sheet covering the mislabeled object to pull it halfway to the floor. A few feet ahead they barely heard the sound of the basket tumble to the ground.

Onward. Onward they ran, dashing past dioramas of Greek Olympics and mystery cults. They sprinted, perhaps unadvisedly, through an area with weapons and armour. They bounded through a short video display of a re-enactment of life in Ancient Greece interspersed with clips of Brad Pitt in the Troy movie.

One more doorway and finally, they arrived.

"Phew!" Laurel took in some air and pressed her hand up against the glass. "Made it."

Adeline arrived a little later and with a surprisingly red face and heavy heaving, she needed a minute before she could look at the object hidden behind the glass, and contributed a hoarse (if appreciative) "Wow."

"Yeah."

Laurel pulled a hammer from her pocket, fresh from the toolbox in the garage.

"Here we go!" she cried, and with a swing...

The glass deflected the carpenter's hammer without so much as a thunk to mark its passing. "Well?" Adeline shrugged.

"I'm trying, Addie! And besides which, I thought you were the athlete here."

Adeline folded her arms. Laurel swung again.

Nothing. Again.

Nothing.

Something splintered off. How it sailed across the space like a cannonball reacting to the explosive force behind it. This was the petty anarchy that made glassmakers grimace and vandals smile. Polished to a shine, the glass grew dull as microfissures expanded enough to be seen by the human eye. Damage enough that lines were made to stream across its fragile surface.

Again.

Something.

Again and she crashed through the glass, falling into the display and catching herself on the object the glass had shielded. She was bleeding where her hands and arms had swept across the crystalline shards.

She burst into tears.

Adeline, looking on, joined her sister and tried to stop

the bleeding by pressing on the areas that were now leaking red, driving the tiny shards further in and earning a few cuts of her own.

Alarms rang out.

They had been too slow.

"Are you –" Adeline had barely begun to ask when the hammer went up once more and came down with all the might a fourteen year old on a quest could muster on a jar that was thousands upon thousands of years old.

If she (or indeed anyone) could have read the Linear A written on the side, maybe her approach might have been less primitive. Perhaps she would have attempted to open the seal from the top.

This was not the case.

The hammer reflected off the surface and sent Laurel backwards into the waiting arms of the drunken (but tragically unrestrained) Fidger. "What in the blue blazes are you doing?" he asked, his voice stern and serious. His hands tightened instantly and then viciously around the vandal.

"I wake to some ropes 'round my arms and feet and this pounding headache to find some ruffians messing about!" He snorted. "Aw, you coulda at least been some of them older kids sneaking around for some nasty. That woulda been forgivable." Laurel was white with fear, and Adeline looked ill.

"The police are on their way, girlies." He stared Adeline down with a resentful gaze that melted into a disgusting, black-toothed grin. "You stay where yer at or your friend here'll get some proper old-world punishing, y' hear?" Adeline nodded.

"No– Addie, you have to open it! Remember the ledger!"

The old man's final gift to the world had been very clear. With red lines and exclamation points around the top. It would have scared them if it hadn't been so intriguing.

Adeline looked to the jar and back at the towering man holding her sister hostage.

"Don't you dare." Fidger shook his head.

"Ow!" Laurel squealed.

"Oh, puddin', it won't leave no mark but I can make things get a lot worse if you don't tell your little 'complice here to stand down!" Adeline lurched forward.

"Now you done it!" Fidger's vise-grip tightened and Laurel's scream echoed through the entirety of the museum's maze-like halls. Adeline's arms were around the Jar. It was nearly her size (and she was tall for fifteen) and her hands struggled to reach the top. She felt the weight of fear and regret fill her, letting fingers swing around the rim, searching for anything to hold onto.

At first they found nothing.

"Do it!" Laurel yelled through the pain. Fidger threw her to the ground and stepped towards the tiny girl in his shadow.

Then, they did.

The pithos opened and out poured...

THE NOVELLA

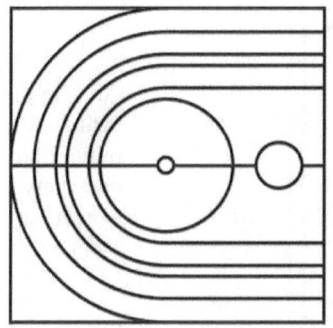

MODERN PHILOSOPHY
A Story About Nobody

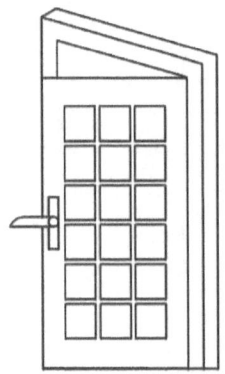

Call me Nobody.
Most people do.

A bit about me so
you can get the right
visuals: I'm thirty-five,
rather plain looking, but
under my calm facade, I'm
a jaded and scattered soul.

I'm already worn
thin. Pathetic, really.

All in all, though,
I feel like I've done a pretty decent job at getting as far away
from the rat races to stop infecting others with my negative
energies and pessimism. Only, in doing so (five years ago
today), I came across something different and wonderful. In
my attempts to escape the hardships of reality, I've entered, as
an intellectual explorer, a distant archipelago that exists on the
fringes of society. If you aspire to understand what I write
here, you deserve to know that these places are real.

Perhaps you deserve to know that you are not alone.
Or maybe when you look back, you will see that I
was only a herald of greater things, of our shared destiny of
chaos and delight.

As I approached the social periphery, my worry
curdled into sour anxiety. Like a gnome standing on the edge
of a flat world lying in a deep fog, I saw nothing in the

bleakness that extended outward beyond what I was told I should believe in. Instead, I felt gnawing thoughts of self-destruction beckoning me to an early grave.

I was prepared to be convinced to jump.

Have you ever felt used and abused?

Have you ever been used and abused?

It starts with the little lies, I'm told.

It starts with things like Santa Claus, and it's punctuated by grandiose, unquantifiable things like dark matter and God and the promise that the future is going to be brighter than the present.

Now, in my depression, I thought to myself: Have I gone too far, become too indifferent to my fellow man? Have I lost touch with what grounds us to the Earth and to one another? What is it to be human – and can it be lost? Must we tear down the canvas of the world to see if anything lay behind it? Do we even dare?

Sometimes we don't.

Take work.

I'm disgusted to the point of physical illness by the prospect of being held to a nine-to-five. I mean, what better encouragement is there to follow up with a cinq-à-sept and perhaps a few more glasses to still the mind and dull the senses?

To make you feel alive again?

If you ever were before.

I used to live for the workweek and dream about the weekend and vacation plans. I used to live in the tomorrow and the days after that. I couldn't appreciate the present.

Yeah, I was stupid back then.

Things make more sense now than they ever did before.

I like to think of it in abstract terms.

As tempting as it might be to believe otherwise, we are gestalt creatures – biologically and psychologically – and what makes up the command centre of our consciousness is sometimes easier to understand as an extensive network – not unlike your own web of friends and family – that unites the personas and phenomena that comprise an identity. It's busier up there than you think.

Let's take a look at my biopsychology as I like to describe it. Let's start with a welcomed newcomer:

My Inner Reality: The Apothecary – Arata

After what happened to… Well, we'll get there. Finding myself in dire need of intellectual and emotional balance, I convened a council of personified psychological states to assist me when I feel too far detached from normalcy.

Near the top of this imaginary inner sanctum and

self-developed psyche-confidants is the venerable Doctor. Oh, I know he's not really a doctor. He's just a figment that helps sort my thoughts. A fact checker. A pencil pusher. A bureaucrat from one end of his governing neurons to the other.

Just a guy who I pretend likes to pressure me into drinking and other tempting debaucheries. A reflection of some strange place where my mind goes when reality becomes too... real.

He's someone I can argue with and feel validated for winning against.

I'm weird like that.

His name is Shinji Arata and he's Japanese. I don't know why, exactly. That's just how I've always pictured him since he manifested. Sometimes, when I close my eyes, I feel like I can see what he's doing: organizing papers and walking through a large, aseptically-white office filled with hundreds of like-dressed men and women, silently going about their days, lost in their tasks and compelled by some near-instinctual drive that only makes sense to them – a reason to eke out their meagre existences.

Doing as they are told.

Obeying some corporate higher calling.

Wearing out and losing themselves to the machinations and the Grand Human Automation Project (GHAP*).

Nah, not really, I just made that up.

Whatever. It's a welcome refuge from the life I live, even if it's a little unnerving how real my mind wants to make it all seem. The power of the imagination is our only true weapon against time and space, boredom and peace, love and hate.

Arata is ordered. He's well-mannered and deadly serious in his commitment to the job. Nothing sways him from his missions. I like to imagine him in slacks and wearing a white shirt and a tie that's just a few tones off from the standard black colour – an exhilarating (albeit subtle) rebellion that differentiates him from the others there. It's the only personality he is allowed, or allows himself. (I'm never quite sure which.) His fellow drones take this stab at individuality as a threat, and as a result observe him with critical, judgmental eyes. Arata relishes the attention, confident they'll never understand how it validates his choices.

In the morning, my evening, I close my eyes and watch as if through his eyes as he hangs his just-black and a bit blue jacket on a chrome hanger and hooks it to the back of his door. He sits at his desk, data filtering in from my mind to be sorted, pouring out through a mechanism something like a printer. There are other machines there, sure, but they're just cosmetic. Arata works for me and he knows it.

He walks slowly through the office while he collates the most important concepts he's collected to be further analysed down the line. Those tiny strides are not done because he is tired or old; instead, it's a product of patient thoroughness. He conserves his energy. He makes himself blend into time and space like black ice on a mountain highway. Like the tide eroding the side of a mountain. He doesn't know that I follow him through these workaday motions in any formal sense, and yet he sorts and suggests and expresses his fears and concerns in a succinct and simple way as if he did. We get along quite well in this respect. This is true even if sometimes I don't quite understand where he gets his conclusions from or how to apply his findings.

Language barrier, probably.

Heh.

Arata, at an automated leisure for which he is known, moves through clogged arteries, analyzing cellular decay, dust in my mind, sore muscles and even recently hurt feelings, then he logs down everything in a ledger that in turn goes into a report on his computer. Everything exists in written and digital format – such is the nature of the bureaucratic system. Sending along the information as his training has specified him to do, he returns to his office and continues his task.

This breakdown of my breaking down covers the basic physical ailments and psychological neuroses that life burdens me with. He usually arrives at the same short-term prescription. He tries to tell me that I'm Normal. Capital-N.

Only… sometimes his advice looks like a fractal of cups and glasses with fine, expensive liquid swimming in clear, clean and shining crystal and it gets worse and more vivid every time I find myself in a depressive spiral. I can feel him insisting that I exceed the recommended dosage for ever-stronger and more liver demanding cure-alls. How advice can taste like fire, I'll never know, but there you have it.

I used to be quite the drunk.

But I can't listen to him anymore.

He's a sick and twisted bastard who, during his off-hours, will sit around and soak up the guilt I feel like a sponge, surviving on the nourishment the angst offers – and then he heads home to his little apartment and sits awake at night, doing unpaid overtime for a boss that probably hates him. We lose our connection in these moments, as if he needs a vacation from me as much as I do from him.

Sometimes, before he goes home, I like to send him out to do karaoke or, if he's lucky, to his family's old home in the countryside, the only maintained building in an abandoned village that was almost entirely swallowed up by the Japanese economic crash a few decades ago.

He vanishes for the duration and we get much-needed time apart.

I'm not crazy.

I don't drink either.

Not anymore.

I'm just bored.

Looking Back: Who I Was – and What I Wasn't

I worked at a university for four years after graduating from a specialized degree program that yielded few real world opportunities. Details don't really matter, and I'm not about to advertise. Experience is what matters. In my time there, I watched mind after mind get warped into a shape that supports the sick orthodoxy of our age.

A way of thinking that insists, time after time after time, that the exploration of new paradigms or the development of new ideas and concepts is wrong.

Unless, of course, you do it their way.

I sat in my office and blanketed my vision with thoughts of elsewhere as the time passed and became the past. I would sit and I would pretend that I could agree with the way things were.

Every time you lie to yourself, that you deny the manifest truth, you lose a little bit of time. Not at the end, or close to the end – rather, you lose time from important experiences that have occurred... or will.

Isn't that a scary thought?

Right?

I even welcomed the opportunity to listen to others complain to me about frivolous things like tuition costs, the state of the world, politics, the promise of youth, the power of the 1%, and a thousand other irrelevancies that swept aside the memories that made me – like the first person I loved and how it all ended.

No, that's not quite right.

I guess I only pretended to listen.

I was lying to these mouthpieces as much as I was lying to myself.

As they spoke, I let myself be carried away on the financial rollercoster (get it?) as I envisioned little boats filled to the gunwales with their tuition destined for the educompanies' vast storehouses, growing the wealth of the aristocracy.

Then I made the dream mine, and watched them burn – tiny Viking funerals for their financial futures. How drôle.

ShapeI shrugged, wondering how many of them knew that the more time they spent in my office, the more their funds dissolved and vanished into a system of education that operates far more like a manufacturing plant than it does a think-tank or a Platonic symposium of knowledge.

Maybe this isn't everyone's experience, but it was mine.

I sat behind a desk, like my inner Arata, and absorbed the life-altering energies of abandoned dreams and forgotten ideas. Sometimes, in the deep of night when the hallways were clear of shuffling feet, sighs, and sweaty armpits, I would take my five wheeled leather chair and ride it from one side of my department to the other with a broom as my oar and... pretend.

Have we all forgotten how to pretend?

Anyway, this is me.

Now, I work down at the Alternative Comedy Club on Some Street. You won't find a sign there. You won't find anything to give you the idea that there's something nefarious or revolutionary happening behind the peeled-purple-paint of what is mistakenly called the English door. Ah, yes, The Door. It's a fun story, so

I'll tell it.

Side story: The English Door – Pimm's Definition

The owner, Pimm, likes to tell the story, so pretend you haven't heard it if it comes up casually in conversation. As far as it goes, his father, a millwright in an area that he will only ever call the Old Country, bought the door when he was traveling through the United Kingdom prior to the big move to North America.

'That's why it's an English door'.

And, to those who dare correct him by suggesting it is, in fact, a French door, be wary lest you join the long and storied list of banned patrons. If he's feeling particularly kind, you'll only receive a warning but your reputation and credibility will carry that tainted mark forever. Pimm can do that. Don't test him.

On the inside, where the hinges have been delicately attached, there's a faded year on the door. 1793, it says. Now, I must address the fact that there's an odd feeling that flows over me when I think of it, knowing that that solitary door has existed on this planet for a period far longer than most of us will count in our lifetime. And, if maintained properly, it will outlive generations more.

It shouldn't be, but I find it awfully strange when I open an ancient door and find, hidden behind it, the present.

Not sure when it became appropriate to give so much credit to a thing but, there it is – and, behind the English door on Some Street, today's most unfathomable minds meet and monologue.

I do stand-up there a few times a week. My show is pretty much an open forum, which isn't uncommon, and rings true for many of my fellow modern philosophers. Interactive shows are real crowd-pleasers, and I love to hear what they have to say when they speak up.

'I think therefore I speak' is my mantra, and while I sometimes get lost along the way, landing far from where I started, that's the beauty of having a job like this one.

But for all my talk of cognitive theory, imaginary businessmen, and the masses' lives of quiet desperation, the place is warm and welcoming, if you can believe it. It's a haven for groups of strangers that unite under an umbrella of intellectualism and healthy debate. It's a speakeasy for a modern age where conformity is the norm, and it is here that the outcasts and the abnormals hold court, their words as sacrosanct as any pagan priest's.

I stand on a small stage with creaking boards and a curtain stained with smoke from a bygone era when such things were tolerated, and I speak into a dusty mic that smells of alcohol, burps, and exotic compounds I couldn't begin to name.

When I'm not on the stage, I recognize the gravity of the old saying: 'Change can be a good thing'.

Like many of the regulars that come down to the club for fun, I welcome the escape it offers from the harsh smog of the city. There's no shame in admitting that I enjoy the VIP status that I have here. I get to sit in the corner booth – the one they reserve for performers – and sip my water while I gather anecdotes from my life and consider what topics would entertain the crowd tonight.

So that's the Alternative Comedy Club, or the ACC.

I'm sure you'll realize that this isn't its true name. I call it that because it sounds stupid. It sounds forgettable. It sounds ridiculous.

It means nothing.

It means something.

But only to those who have experienced it before.

How can that be? There are certain things that we are able to take on the mere word of others and accept them to be real. Then, there are other things that defy description – people, places, and experiences too unique to comprehend without shared context.

Without initiation.

The ACC is such a place.

Some call it the Ministry. Either could be right. Both might be wrong.

I'm confident enough in your deductive abilities to assume you've already figured out that the name of the street is likewise probably not Some Street, either.

Even if I were willing to provide you with directions, which I am not, I think you'll appreciate and recognize (those of you who get it, I mean) what the place is really called.

Character Profile: The Neuronaut – Capital J.

I sit in my corner waiting for the end of this last bulwark of beatnik culture to complete his time in the limelight. He turns to me and gives a knowing nod, and laughs in a way that forces you either join him or scrunch up your face because of the way the decibels uniformly assault your eardrums. He wears clothes that have become trendy again, but that's not intentional; the old saw about a broken clock comes to mind. It would be fair to believe that he hasn't bought anything new in a decade or more.

I can't tell you how many times people have called him a hipster and how he just smiles and nods back. He has no idea what that means.

Hipster is not a new word, to be sure, but even to him it's something that's out of reach for one reason or another. If one were to explain to him what it meant, he would claim that he's so sequestered from modern trends that he could not possibly be a hipster.

Rejecting the title – the very concept – out of hand.

Ironically, that only deepens his hipster cred.

He thinks his tie-dye shirt and bowler cap that matches well with his book of Hemingway-inspired poetry means he has things worked out just fine. He smiles with a crooked grin that he earned in a war, but none that you would have heard of – many question its existence at all, but never in his presence.

Not after last time.

Jones is the name he goes by. Or, for whatever reason, Capital J.

Calamity and Confusion: An Orchestra – Regular
Players

Now, Jones has been around since the ACC was still held in the off-hours at a mechanic's garage over on Any Avenue. (No clues, as promised). Back before they found this place, built up the inside and stuck the English door on the front. He, like me, doesn't drink. I guess we have that much in common.

He calls me Uncle Adam.

Well, for a while I thought he was saying that.

I didn't look into it much because, I have to say, it freaked me out. I just couldn't figure out how he'd discovered that nugget of who I was and wasn't prepared to believe that he knew even more. Eventually, when I got my own slot at the ACC, I arrived and checked the evening's schedule, and found that someone (Capital J, I presume) had scratched out my name and written Uncial Adam in its place.

Yeah. Had to look that one up.

I don't get it.

I wonder if even he does.

He might not drink, but Capital J sure loves to get down with the psychoactives.

"They get my head on straight. They get me out of bed in the morn'ng. If I got cut off I'd probably just lie down right here and die." He starts some of his sets with a few grams of mushrooms and a drop or two of acid. I'm always impressed how collected he manages to be by the end.

People like him because he's willing to share and leaves a bag and an eyedropper on the chair at the front of the stage. Whenever someone comes up to partake he pulls them to the stage and asks them for a story. He doesn't care about quality – he just wants to hear what other people say.

We also have that in common.

Capital J, Pimm told me when I got my regular spot, is apparently

a very rich man. Like, this guy can apparently afford to keep a small contingent of gold diggers following him around and praising his every word. Even if he's never been known to share his wealth with anyone apart from, well, the obvious.

Persistence is a virtue, I suppose.

Maybe they're just hoping that he'll grow tired of his lonesome existence and accidentally let on about where his fortune is hidden – and it is hidden, that much is as certain as rumour can be.

'We're talking own-a-small-island-nation level of fortune here, pal,' is the way Pimm likes to describe him. Personally, I'm a bit on the fence about the whole thing. Any piece of gutter-trash would tell you the same if they thought it might grab your attention or earn them a drink, and while Capital J is not one to brag about his personal finances, there is a je ne sais quoi element about the man that I quite admire.

The story Pimm goes on to tell is that Capital J doesn't really use his fortune much anymore because of the fact that it was built on tragedy, and the way he chooses to live is a weird penance for contributing so negatively to the world.

He single-handedly pays for Pimm's ACC. Some even suggest that they are actually a couple, and to that I say good for them if it's true, and even if not, at least they seem to support one another. Together, the two have worked to open clubs like it across the country with varying levels of success. There are apparently a few overseas as well, but they have... geographical... managers, or something like them (your guess is as good as mine – I can't imagine any of them having board meetings or signing off on quarterly reports), so we don't hear much about them. If I had to guess I'd say there are probably fifteen or twenty ACC affiliates across this strange, stupid world of ours.

At the end of a day, or the beginning of his act, Capital J remains a man difficult to quantify. I like that about him. On the other hand, there are characteristics and habits that are sometimes so overwhelmingly bad that they almost undo the elements that work in his favour.

For example:

Sometimes, after three or four days straight on the clock and on the stage, his clothes become soaked in so much sweat that they practically become building material. At which point Pimm will guide him back to the changing room and ask him to go home and the man will just sit there and cry for a while – or have a spell, as Pimm calls these occasions.

As in, "He's having one of his spells again."

You can't really hide much in the ACC. The place isn't very big and the sound carries. So whether you're taking a particularly devastating shit in the single-stall unisex toilet or you're heading into an emotionally crippling bad trip, people are probably going to hear you. Silly old man. He has to know.

After a good cry, he'll head out to front and always – and I mean always – the same black car will pull up and help him into the back. This is why I say that I'm on the fence about who Capital J really is. The answers are probably easy enough to find, but I don't really care enough to uncover them. He is who he is just as I am who I am.

Character Profile: The Owner – Pimm

He's a raggedy man with enough charisma and lingering good looks that he must have been quite the popular guy back in the day. I'm not trying to suggest that people who come to the ACC don't commonly possess these attributes, just – well, if you met Pimm you would understand.

I hope you get to meet him.

His voice is deep and welcoming. His eyes are exact and analytical, his humour precise and his wit dry as a desert. He's the type of person you want to have at your parties – be they fancy, casual, or more difficult to categorize. Stories flow through him like they've just thawed off a glacier, with a timeless, bardic reverence that catches the attention and captures the mind. His office is at the back of the ACC's nook. Technically speaking it's not inside the ACC building at all, but a canopied alleyway where the top neighbouring buildings come close to touching, fail, and instead form a hidden area.

Some of the older ACC vanguards say that it is the result of an earthquake.

I've never heard of earthquakes here, though.

Overlapping rings left by neglected glasses decorate his fine old mahogany desk, with intricate symbols and Chinese pearl inlay.

People who were around in the beginning call him President Pimm, a title we hear less and less as more of them meet their makers. I can't quite place his age. I doubt it would be uncharitable to place him in his late eighties, if not well older than that.

Despite the stories he shares, few seem to be personal, and so I've gotten to know him more through his daughter than I have the man himself. He's kind, though, and I can tell that there are things on his mind even when he seems focused on the present.

Character Profile: The Violent Lady – Gae

One of the best parts about working at the local ACC, for me at least, is getting to know Pimm's daughter: Megaera, or just Gae. Strictly off-limits, she is the hot commodity that brings in the thirsty crowd from late to very late.

(Also early morning, if you're the sort that cares about fine distinctions like that.)

Now, it would be impolite to say that she's anything less than a vision, but it's her intellect that is her true gift.

But to be impolite: She's devastatingly, mind-blowingly, incomparably Hot.

She has short red hair and dark brown skin that almost ignites the dark atmosphere that reigns in our humble hole-in-the-wall. We've known each other for five years and in that time, I'd like to say that I listened to the house rules on keeping away but that wouldn't be true. We matched well enough in the beginning, as so many tragic relationships do. Then, over just a few weeks, we went from whirlwind romantics to catastrophically incompatible. I can't really point to any one cause. On paper, as in thought, we match like two sides of a puzzle. In practice, we were as similar as water and oil. It just came to a point where I would close my eyes and wish she was gone. I did it so often that eventually, she was.

I don't regret it.

We're friends now, and that story arc is in the past, so I won't trouble you with it.

I was more sensible back then, and after we desynchronized I fell into a great depression and fed myself on an even deeper anger. Arata and various other psychological constructs were put into place to help me cope. They've played as great a part in my creative evolution as they have on my character, and for that reason I can look back now, after the storm has passed, and see that all of it was good.

So yeah, maybe I do regret it a bit.

Gae, as her name suggests to the ear, is joyous, and one of a kind.

She's with a young artist these days who does pretty well for himself, and she seems happy and we still talk and hang out when I'm doing sets at the ACC.

Her father brought her into the fold of the ACC when

she was only fifteen and at thirty-three she's seen a lot of what this side of the wall looks like. Her ability to carry on conversations about Marxist idealism or debate the ethical and moral implications of animal testing before human trials, all through a three AM haze of smoke, speaks volumes about the impression the place has had on her, and that she in turn has had on the ACC. What did she always say before I started a set? That's it – raise the discourse. An admirable goal.

She's a vegan, too, if that means anything to some of you.

Didn't make much of a difference to me, but I can't fight my upbringing and my cravings. This is a flaw that I expend as much energy fighting against as Goliath did against David. You think you should be able to win but alas, sometimes the unexpected occurs and you find yourself with late-night quinoa cravings and a comprehensive understanding of what constitutes a "superfood". That's Gae for you.

She volunteers at a local medical clinic and helps with vaccinations, piss tests, and other routine procedures. Pimm says she was studying medicine before her mother died and that the tragedy derailed her, leaving her driverless in her own life.

Leaving behind the old and reinventing herself, Gae was swept into a new stream of purpose by her desire to escape.

She didn't have to go far.

Bartending at the ACC pays the bills, while her performances bring in enough people that she's purchased a few apartments across the city to rent out to the riffraff. Or so she likes to claim.

To my knowledge, I'm the only riffraff.

Her father thinks she's entrepreneurial, but doesn't realize the apartments have been carefully converted into grow-ops for, no surprises here, her boyfriend.

I'd say that at least ninety percent are used for this purpose. I'm sorta her charity case, and she lets me pay late or, sometimes, when a month is hard, not at all. Can't fault a person like that – especially if you're the one benefiting from the situation. It would be unseemly. Even rude.

So about her boyfriend. Just because he's one of the biggest dealers this side of the river doesn't mean he can't also be a real quality character. He pays his taxes. He supports non-profits. He pickets asinine new laws and publicly advocates for sensible policies. Mostly, he just tries to be visible. What better way to hide than in plain sight? But seriously. He's a nice guy – sends regular alimony checks and child support payments to his ex-wife, and takes an active role in raising the kids (one that's his, two that aren't) whenever he can. So what if he's sitting on hundreds of thousands of dollars in thoroughly whitewashed cash collected from desperate psychonauts starving for their next glimpse of the divine mechanism that binds reality together and keeps humans so far apart?

Doesn't bother me in the least.

Oh, I'm not very good at lying, am I?

There's a lot to be said about Gae – too much, really.

She likes strange things and gets excited about harrowing subjects like measles outbreaks or impending world-altering political decisions. There are no Barbies in her closet or visions of white dresses in her future. She's stepped sideways from convention and shot at expectations with both barrels of her imaginary sidearm (sometimes literally; she's an unusually talented mime with a flair for combat).

Her armpits are hairy and her legs well-insulated, and that's all good because she's a damn fine person. I like Gae because she's one of the few who can wrest the course of a conversation away from me, even when I'm on a roll.

You came here for a different reason, though.

You want to hear the weird stories.

The ones that make your spine tingle and warp your sense of perspective, that strip you of the illusions and assumptions that let you sleep. Goodness knows why, but you want to peer over the abyss without the safety railing, to lock your ego in a shiny tin box while the universe shows you just how small you really are.

You want to walk the line and learn what made me forget the petty rules of civilization, how I replaced the flimsy fabric of social convention with my own, albeit jaded perspective. I'll start with a story that I think will pierce the veil that clouds the eyes of our kinsmen.

This is one of my favourite performances. When I travel to a new city I go straight to the online boards and find the nearest ACC. Sometimes, when I know where I'm going before I set off on a journey, I'll even call ahead and see if I can book an evening or two on their stage, offering my services and lend my arrogance to the ambience. So, here we go:

Traveling Oddities: My Other City – Oh, How it

Shimmers

There's a story (or a myth, or a fable, or a folktale) that they like to tell in a city by the sea. It comes out differently every time but has one solid focus – there's a place that once found can never be found again.

You're probably wondering how that's possible, like I did, but this is not a story for smartasses who think that there are shortcuts to enlightenment. So while you fight to suspend disbelief, let me return to the description of this terrible place. Triumphant, in a way, how it fights against the natural order. Against roads that work both ways. Against stories that end. Can you imagine a time before the City – for there is only one – sprawled like a rusted mould across the face of the world? Before humanity burned through habitats and dug through mountains to sate the hunger in its heart? To displace. To enclose. To civilize.

But as greedy as the City is, it freely shares its hunger, as more and more people elect for modern convenience over... well, whatever life they could have had elsewhere.

The City reaches towards the skies with towers of shimmering light that cut through the darkness – not with the life-giving warmth of a campfire, but the cold glint of a knife. A sunless night, as bright as day – and while the inner-animal denies me the mercy of contentment, I can see how the glass and the steel are beautiful in their own way. It's a monument to industry where, when the evening has gone and the factories spring to life, smog billows over the rooftops while air conditioning units make war on warm summers and mild winters.

The City by the Sea is not the legend it carries, but they have much in common.

Once you find the legend, you can never find it again.

But once the City finds you, you can never leave.

I fucking hate this place.

The people move with an impatience that manifests in bitter invectives, car horns, and frantic fingers that wave back and forth at targets aware or otherwise. The beds stink of humanity. The sun is lost behind concrete structures until noon, when it casts its rays directly down like a magnifying glass burning ants.

I come back because I can't seem to leave, and because it's always halfway between where I was and where I'm going. And maybe it isn't all that bad. I don't mind the weather and the ACC here is good.

So: it was here, after one night spent on stage offering my anecdotes and observations that I was approached by a white-as-a-sheet woman with blue bangs and bleached-blonde hair cut into a star-shape that hung down over her ears and arced over the back of her head.

In this way she rather looked like Sonic the Hedgehog if he was depressed and anemic. With boobs. And slightly more human proportions. And clothes on (at least in the beginning).

Hmmm.

Revision: Her hair looked like a woven starfish, closing its arms around her head.

That's a bit better, but not great.

All the same, it fit her in a weird sort of way.

"I liked your set." she said, her voice miniscule and quiet. "My name is Rama." She gave a low bow that, I presumed, meant she was a complete bastard, trying to seem dignified, or, and as it was confirmed, had some cultural entitlement to it. The name made my inner science fiction aficionado laugh: Here I am, having a Rendezvous with Rama.

I didn't mention this.

I told her my name and she offered to buy me a drink. We got to talking and after five, maybe six drinks total, she started to get into her life story. I don't remember everything, only that she was somehow selected from a group of people working at an affiliated Alternative Comedy Club in Wakayama Prefecture in Japan to take her show on tour in the United States.

They paid for her trip, and she had such a good time that she decided to stay, revising her act for North America and working on new sets. She didn't look very young, but the ACC seems to attract both old souls and the inexplicably ageless, and it's so hard to tell with Asian people – and believe me, I don't mean that as a racist comment! I mean that as the purest compliment to those who can maintain the blush of youth until suddenly, youthful becomes venerable.

I already look older than I should, but that's part of a longer story, just one that hasn't become relevant yet.

Addiction: The Boon – The Bane

"We should go see the Dorman." She was hiccupping when she said it and her accent made itself known. "Have you ever seen it?"

I recall shrugging. "What's a Dorman?"

She just smiled and took me by the hand. I was in no position to disagree with her and the events that followed would mark the beginning of my lasting sobriety. I can't remember it with any clarity and that's the problem. I didn't have Arata back then to chastise me by making me feel like I should be drinking. So, on that night and many others besides, I just drank and drank without thinking much about it.

Like so: I didn't need anyone to tell me that I should be drinking. I just liked to drink.

So I did.

A lot.

The world was only visible to me like a fish in an aquarium. Before I could compose myself we were out the back of the ACC and into a cab. She pounced on me the moment the car started rolling – to the disgust of the driver who, after a few minutes, pulled over and demanded we pay the fare in advance. I reached for my pocket but she stopped me.

"I've got this." She leaned forward, pulled money from her neon bra and handed it to the man in the driver's seat. "Do we have your permission to continue?" she asked, sarcastically.

He shrugged and started driving again.

I wish I had looked outside and watched where we were heading but I was… occupied. There's a vague sense now, as I lay awake at night and wonder about that place and look at maps trying to calculate what road we may have taken. I did remember in the end, but was at a loss for what I would find upon my return.

By the time we arrived I was already tiring of her youthful energy. Traveling so much takes a toll on a person. I wanted to curl up on a bed and let dreams carry me off to places unseen and unimagined.

Rama asked the driver to kindly fuck himself as she slammed the door and pulled me along, laughing and screaming as if no one could hear us there. Looking around, she was probably right. Against all odds, we were out of the sprawl. The stars were dim but visible – that much I remember.

She handed me something and told me to swallow.

I obeyed, unthinking, and in moments my mind was on fire.

Time warped and shifted. Patterns grew and dissolved.

"We're here!" The blurred woman ahead of me, like a silhouette cutting across a static background like in those old Saturday morning cartoons, jumped and glided down the edge of a hill.

She had said as much, but I knew we were there.

Whatever the Dorman was… I found myself drawn

to the gravitational pull of a single, shining point of blackness behind us, marred by the merest imperfection in its depths. It stuck out of the scene like a swollen tumour. Like a fallen star cut into the Earth, held captive within a stony mound where the grass stopped growing and a cave's mouth that seemed to lick its lips at our arrival.

I couldn't see the ocean but the smell of salt and the sound of crashing waves suggested it wasn't far off.

"What... Beauty is this?" I asked, my voice distorted. It wasn't the right word. I wanted to leave.

She leapt up at me again and planted a dry-lipped kiss on the widening gyre of my expression. I wanted to look ahead but we drifted down to the soft soil and I simply lost the will to fight.

"This is a sacred place. A timeless place. They say that everything ends, Nobody, but..." She was suddenly distant. "Why are we here?" she asked me, looking tired and very confused.

"You brought me here...?" I was worried I'd said the wrong thing, but she smiled and licked her lips with a serpentine tongue pierced with a–

"Is that a compass?" I asked her, staring into her mouth.

"Yessss." She stuck it out for me to see. "Do ooh like it?" Her pronunciation was pretty good, considering she was literally tongue tied.

"Why is it spinning?" I watched the needle run amok.

"Is it broken?"

Her pierced eyebrow went up.

"It should work. It used to, at least."

I shrugged it off. "Whatever." I turned over to get a better look at the anomaly that had never quite stopped pulling on the back of my head. "So, how did you find out about this place?" We were so close to the blackness that I felt like it was going to reach out and touch me.

"Three years ago... I saw a map drawn on one of the bathroom stall walls at the Wakayama ACC. By the time I was sober enough to realize what I'd seen, someone had already scraped it off. I have a good memory, though. It wasn't hard to recognize this city, and it wasn't hard to redraw. Once I got them to put me on a plane, it didn't take long to find it. I visited once a few weeks ago. I didn't want to come alone. I wasn't supposed to."

The world might have been melting, but none of it seemed to touch her. She looked so innocent. But this drugess, if you'll excuse the neologism, was nothing of the sort.

"Why are we here?" she asked again.

"Are you okay, Rama? You've asked that, like, two times already.

You brought me here."

She sighed. Obviously, I was failing interdimensional orientation.

"NO! Not here. I mean here. I listened to your stories about university, about work, about everyone being the same and they all gave me this... chill. I knew that there was something about you. I knew that you would be able to understand why I needed to go – and look!" She perked up. "We're here! Just like I thought we would be!" Her smile went as wide as the Cheshire Cat's.

I was tripping balls.

And that's an understatement.

The air, the earth, the matter around the vine-covered hole at the centre of the Dorman looked to be the only thing that wasn't about to catch fire, but I held back that suspicion because Rama looked perfectly calm.

Even if I did find myself distracted by the fact that she was also beginning to look even more like a cat.

"I don't know why we're here, Rama." I said, quietly, resting my head on her chest. She was warmer than I expected, but her heart was beating at a calm, collected, and precise rate. The natural music of a natural instrument.

"Good," she offered.

"It's good to be good." My mind wasn't allowing for much in the way of profound conversation. The pull from the anomaly was undeniable and deeply uncomfortable, but I had allowed whatever part of me that carried me through situations I couldn't abide – lectures, meetings, funerals – to take charge. To its great credit, it was still using all of its processing power to make sure I appeared as interested in her, and her alone, as possible.

The rest of me, however, was desperately working to ensure I didn't start losing my mind.

"How about we be bad?" Her teeth were a mile-wide, shining like a jagged cave of diamond.

This is where the night took a turn for the weird.

Not the drugs, or the isolation, or the woman I had only encountered just hours before, but something was approaching at breakneck speed that was going to... Well, I didn't know.

Have you ever felt the cold, faceless future come up to you with a look that demands your attention and informs you, in no uncertain terms, that you've done something very wrong?

The Future and I shared a lasting gaze that let me know it knew what I was going to do and wasn't pleased about it. I recall it every day. I recall that morning. I recall it the moment that I get out of bed and feel the flow of electricity streaming from every inch of my home... and I do my best to shrug it off and get with the program.

If I were a religious man, I might perceive the sensation as some kind of omen, like the herald of some grand plan that begins to unfold there and then.

And before I can forget what I feel, what I know, I am reminded of an image on the roof above the altar at the church I attended when I was younger and still naive. It depicted an angel shattering the lock on a cloud-seated brass doorway. "The Welkin Gate", they called it.

The movement captured in that painting was a testament to the power of an artist that believed in the work he had been set to do. Even as you looked closer, and even though you knew it was all a trick of the light, the angel's golden hammer drew ever closer to the lock. As if at that very moment – at every moment – it would finally break and unleash all the celestial brilliance held within.

That was how I felt then. It has never left me.

Energy flowed out of the dark spot and cut through me as the moonlight pierced the canopy of a tall ash tree not too far away. I gasped as I heard wood splinter in my chest.

As a child, looking at the mural, I was inspired – even if the image, I was constantly reminded, was an interpretation of the doorway to heaven rather than the real thing. There were no passages in the Bible that suggested an angel was going to break the seal to paradise.

I wonder, though, to this very day: Why was it locked from the outside? And by whom?

Rama was ahead of me, and she looked like the very image of a fallen goddess.

I drew a deep breath and the world, as I believed it was going to, burst into flames around us.

Without a thought, we took each others hands and ran.

We had drifted away from the Dorman somehow, but the return trip was faster than I expected – or perhaps I'd just never run with fire at my back. But sure enough, the shimmering field offered protection from the elements. We fell to the grass and struggled to catch our breath, and somewhere along the way we started kissing. In the light of a world on fire, we wrapped ourselves up in one another – and tearing through our clothes and every lie we'd ever told, it wasn't long until we were breathless again.

That Place – The Trouble with Perception

Something opened.

Pulled from that spot of deep light, we floated or soared or screamed our union and forgave ourselves for getting carried away.

The darkness drew us in and together we fell. Down into the veins of the world and through their winding, chaotic passages to somewhere else. Hands became steel jaws snapping at my throat; stars pulse in my chest; Rama's breasts lay just out of reach, only to be replaced by lidless eyes and crying laughter I couldn't recognize.

It must have been the acid.

If it was acid at all.

It could just as easily been some newly-imagined or ancient fármako that should never have been. All I know is that I had never tried it before, and in the throes of being torn apart by pain and pleasure (I really wish I had been able to tell the difference) I was struck by how abjectly unprepared I'd been for the things I'd seen and done.

I can remember screams – but I still can't remember if they were inspired by terror or orgasm.

Sometimes, even after all these years, I have out of body experiences and feel like I'm being pulled back through to that place.

Inside: I Met a Lightblue Dick – The Tetranne

I walked through a kaleidoscope and watched as Rama and I separated into two, joined together into one, and fell apart once more as our minds measured reality and reality grasped to understand US.

Colours started to take shape around us. Not just any shape. Human shape. Things that were distant and uncertain took on structure, focus, and proportions that made sense to me.

At first there was a flat surface. A horizon.

It warped and from it, like Genesis in fast-forward, terrain sprang up and changed the perfect plane into something new – but not too different from where we had just been. A tree (or something near enough in size and shape to a tree) was the first to arise, as a deep magenta colour spread across the ground and into the distance. The tree was blue, with greenish leaves shaped like small triangles.

I looked around and found myself alone. Alone and… translucent.

Note: This isn't precisely what happened next. I could tell you the story as I experienced it, the sounds I heard, the people I met, and the emotions I felt, but it would fall on deaf ears. Let the madman on the corner tell the story true; I'll do you the courtesy of meeting you halfway.

I stood up and found it easy, as if I didn't so much need to get up as I needed to think that I needed to get up, and my body reshaped itself into that position. On the ground, cuttingly through a broad field of blue moss-like foliage, small footprints went off and away.

Looking around, I saw that this side of Dorman was polarized. At the centre of the shimmering circle was a single black spot, but it had no gravity of its own. In fact, I felt pushed away. Naturally, I took the opportunity to stare at it for a while. Call me contrary.

Where Are We: What... What the FUCK?!

I followed the footprints in the coloured soil. Trailing away from the Dorman, the steps started off tentative, then spread out into a run, but after a while, they slowed and became more collected. I'm no Boy Scout on Earth, but those tracks spoke as clearly of a quick victory over panic as any relieved confession. I just wish I could tell you how..

It was beautiful, though. The geometric edges had faded from the world, and tall fleshy trees danced in the absence of wind. The sky, a grayish shimmer, almost like the reflection off of a metal surface. It looked like an old film. It reminded me of Casablanca, dull yet undeniably alive. Sound here was different. Rather than fading gradually, sounds seemed to be locked to the objects that produced them, with consistent volume until you stepped outside an imperceptible sphere of influence. Then silence.

This, I noticed when I approached a... well, it would be stupid to call things here strange or weird. They certainly seemed unreasonable by my old standards, but fucking your way into another dimension has a way of redefining one's standards of normality.

Note: The ground, where Rama's feet had left her trail, had already started to return to its original shape. Stranger still, insofar as I could tell, all the footprints seemed to lose definition together, denying their own creation in service of some natural law I couldn't begin to comprehend.

The fresher footprints before me should have lasted longer than the ones I was leaving behind, and yet, even as I glanced back, I saw all of them sponging back to their original contours simultaneously.

Like a memory-foam pillow after a quick nap. I never did like those things.

I said before that the ground was squishy in texture, almost like with sufficient pressure I might be able to puncture the surface and find whatever was underneath, like a film or a biomass.

There was a darker possibility, too, and this one kept me moving forward – that if I waited too long, the ground would swallow me up like the footprints. Well, not swallow per se, more like absorb.

I still have difficulty finding the right words for that place.

"RAMA!" I called out but there was no carry to my voice. Whatever laws were in charge here were prepared to assert themselves on me as well.

Location: The Spiral City – Reddal

I couldn't tell you how long I walked but finally, in the distance, I spotted a grand spiralling object peek its pointed top over the tentacled forest. It looked like what would happen if you took a common tower shell – you know, the type you find on the beach or in those cheesy movies where people put them up to their ears and listen for the ocean? – smoothed out the curve and added, well, I guess it was the closest thing to a building I'd seen yet.

Flashforward: Philosophy – The Plan

I was standing a fair distance from the structure ahead of me when I heard the strangest voice cry out "You there! Stop!" These were red words, and I knew I had to run...

Let me jump forward a bit.

To an abandoned painter's (our word, not theirs) studio on the outskirts of Reddal, the capital city of the Chroma Imperium. I and my newfound friend LightBlue were shixing – which is to say, we were talking about what to do next. While it was an odd enough experience to be where I was, absorbing and accepting the experience with such ease was something else entirely.

The longer I was exposed to the environment, the more I found that words and concepts that defy the unbroken mind were suddenly mine to understand.

I looked at the space above – the sky – and I knew that they called this time of the daily cycle that I now call, in an attempt to translate it to English as best as I can, the Whither. I knew, too, that in some time it would transition to the Grather, and, finally, in a darkness like our night, we would experience the Nether – from white to gray to black.

As much as it horrified me to know this all by instinct, it was fascinating.

I would hear a piece of information that I had never known before and, almost instantaneously, I would understand the context. I think the same was true for him, and that was why our friendship formed so quickly, despite the fact that neither of us had ever encountered anyone quite like the other. (That didn't bode well for finding Rama, but I kept that context to myself.)

In the short time we had been together, he'd already helped me evade the forces of the Nearest Primary and had put himself at odds with his own people as a result. I didn't fully understand the debt that I owed him then, or at least, I wasn't prepared to acknowledge it just yet.

I knew that I owed him my life, at least.

"Anom," he said, refusing to make eye contact, first looking at his drink and then back into the distance with a sunken expression that, as with so many things on the Tetranne, has proven impossible to accurately describe.

I'll do my best to translate. The phrase "you had to be there" has never applied to you more than it does now.

"Anom. We have a story here." He laughed awkwardly; LightBlue wasn't a raconteur by nature. "No. It's not a story. It's a promise. It comes from the Highest Authority. From the very PRISM before we Chromas came to exist here. Do you care to hear it?"

"Of course." I was sitting at the edge of my seat waiting for whatever he had to say – well, say might be wrong word for a being without a mouth, or at least none that I could see. It's not that he had any trouble sipping his drink (which was delicious, by the way, and you'll find my best attempt to replicate it on the menu of your favorite local ACC), but it just kind of disappeared halfway between his nose and his chin. But besides that and his... picturesque pigmentation, LightBlue was as human as anyone I'd ever met. And just like me, he was a being of stories.

"Long ago there was a book. Many hold to the belief that the Chromatome was not written. That it formed from all the colours that the PRISM released that did not coalesce into the Tetranne, our world. I am not so sure of this, but it is what my people profess to believe. So few are allowed to gaze upon it nowadays that some have become... suspicious. Chromas like myself. We theorize that it doesn't exist at all, that it never did. It doesn't matter what may be the case – Fact or Fiction – for it is Faith that has driven our society." He stopped to see that I was listening.

"I follow you. Go on." And, as I said earlier, strangely, I did follow him. I understood the importance of what he was saying and even how it fit into their world.

"The Nearest Primaries have long claimed the right to Blending Authority. One cannot simply create a new Chroma without first being vetted for your potential to break the First Rule of Eight. This, you must understand, is the cornerstone of our society, and its eightfold perfection grants us the peace that has endured since the Disjunction. The First Rule, Nobody, it concerns you and is the likely cause of the commotion in Reddal. " He took a breath, or the Chroma equivalent. "The First Rule is this: colour must be preserved at all costs. It is said that the Chromatome, real or not, speaks of the end of the world, and that it will be heralded by the creation of a Non-Colour." He let me think about that for a moment.

I didn't need a moment – in fact, I'd just as soon forget the way that word seemed to draw the air from my lungs – but he didn't wait very long before continuing.

"This is why unauthorized blending and creation means execution at the hand of the Nearest Primaries: the force of prophecy. Of superstition. You see, no one haS ever created anything but another Chroma. The Blending Authority says that this is only true because they have made it so, but I say it is a regime of death built on false pretenses." He paused again.

"Ever since our first encounter I have thought that there was something strange about you. You are not a colourless and yet... you are not a Chroma either. I wonder..."

I sprang to my feet with the sudden knowledge that Rama was in danger. "We have to find her!" I shouted, my mind ready to will myself into motion, but LightBlue would have none of it. He waved his hand and beckoned me to sit with the same calm demeanour that had won me over when we first met.

"I know where she is. They will have taken her to the Tower. Where they take all who dare defy them. It is near the base of Reddal, but it is heavily guarded and despite that... I want to help you."

"Why?"

"Not all of us agree with the Nearest Primaries or their brutal enforcers. Some of us have expressed interest in returning to our ancestral lands, but the Red Army continues to occupy them 'for our own protection', for 'unity'. It's all lies. They experiment on us, Nobody, with the Nearest Primaries' blessing. They defile our bodies in a sadistic hope that we will somehow restore our True Colours."

"True Colours?"

"We are... fading. All of us. If we are not careful, we will continue to lose our essence, our... being... and we will become like the Tonelands, gray and soulless. The Authority has forbidden me from taking a mate because I am of the Light family, which has been judged and found lacking. I will be the last of my kin. I once accepted this for fear that what they say is true, and that our world will fall if a Non-Colour is born. But you... you are not of the Tetranne. If you truly come from another world, well, perhaps there are other places that will accept a faithless Chroma like me." He smiled and leaned in, and his voice grew quiet.

"There is another legend, like that of the Chromatome. It is old and it is blasphemous to even mention, yet those who know it all too well. It says that there are doorways hidden across the world, perhaps through which our ancestors once travelled to this place. They say that when we came here we were all... without colour or form. That these things came later. I wonder if, long ago, we were the same, your people and mine."

It was a sad story, and LightBlue had my sympathy, but his timing left much to be desired. "How is any of this going to save my friend?" I asked, springing back to my feet. I didn't need tales and theories, I needed action – and every second we waited was another one that put Rama closer to her death.

"First. You will tell me about who you are and then I will help you."

"Are you fucking kidding me?" I was ready to leave then and there, but there was that calmness again... and despite my best attempts to tell him in no uncertain terms exactly what he could do with his little therapy session, I told him. It didn't take too long, after all – probably just another principle of the Tetranne that isn't true here on Earth. After that, he sighed and stood up.

"Ah. You are one like the Translucents of myth. Now that I understand the paths you traveled to get here, I see that I was correct, that you are not a colourless, but the others… They would see you as a threat to the very existence of our world. As they have probably perceived your friend."

It echoed our initial meeting, this tone of his, when he had launched himself at me without provocation or questioning. I swore and I tried to get him off of me, but his hands and feet were quicker than mine and far more precise. Strangely, though, his strikes did not hurt as much as I would have expected them to. It was almost as if the very nature of pain in this place had a different texture.

All the same, and pain aside, it had been quite the fight.

Eventually, when I had him pinned and we began to speak… or whatever it was… (it seemed like speaking, at least) we started to evaluate the situation and, yeah, I told him enough about my day that he grew interested in my well-being.

He'd been kind to me ever since.

If not also incredibly curious and stricken by the news that there were other stable worlds through the Dorman. Several forbidden tales later, I learned there were actually tons of them at one point. If the Tetranne had given me nothing else, it was a healthy trust in the value of apocrypha.

Most of these worlds, if not all of them, were thought to have been destroyed well before recorded history. During a time they called the Purge. It might have been that our common ancestors were trying to escape… something.

Details are sparse.

Somehow, Earth and the space near our Dorman survived.

He says I came through the Divide. An area that's deadly to the Chromas, a phenomenon that's likely responsible for its continued existence.

"How are we going to save her?"

"We are going to do what I was trying to do when we met. We are going to walk you to the Agents of the Near Primaries and they are going to take you to the Tower. I will rally my friends, those who I know are loyal, and we will rescue you. I have spent some time in the Tower, in what was a lifetime ago, and my captors have much to answer for." He reached out and touched my shoulder, blue incandescent light shining through my body. "You must take me with you. I cannot stay in this place, and if I am to retrieve you from the Tower I will need to know that there is a chance for me elsewhere."

"I don't even know if we can go back."

"If we find the way back to your Dorman, will you take me?"

"Yeah, sure, why not." Now that the stories had ended, I don't think time was moving the same way anymore, and that made me worried about Rama. "Shouldn't we get going?"

"I have no doubt that your friend will be made an example of. They will keep her alive until they unblend her.

That will be in the WhiteTone."

That was a few days away, at least.

"We will need to plan and I will need to speak with my contacts. If not for their help, you may become just another victim of our corrupt and inflexible system."

Flashforward: The Escape – Up Shit's Creek

"Don't look back!" LightBlue yelled, audibly and visibly distressed as we rushed over the edge of the Tower's wall and slid down the hill towards his compatriot, a freshly defected Agent of the Near Primaries: PaleRed.

"Where are the others?"

I already knew the answer.

Rama, in my arms, was still and quiet. I didn't know if she was even alive before she grunted when we hit the ground. Even when I swept her up from the cell floor, she hadn't made a sound. I could work with a grunt.

"They'll have their skylancers on us in no time. We'll make it to the rendezvous point and then we'll have to make a break for your doorway."

It does sound like "door", doesn't it? The thought hadn't occurred to me yet, and it came as a surprising relief for little things to replace the larger, horrifying truth that we were being hunted by living colours that were willing to die if it meant killing us.

The four of us that had made it out of the Tower were united in a common bond of desperation and well-founded faith in legends and rumours of worlds beyond.

PaleRed's head was... bleeding? I don't know how to describe it better than to say that she was looking a few scales pinker than she had when we met back in the interrogation room. Without her there would have been no chance.

"Are you okay?"

She shot me a glare that said absolutely not, fuck you very much and I shut up until the spiral city had faded into tentacle forest. We were back to the old painter's house not far from where LightBlue first punched his way into my circle of friends.

Oh, the adventures we had.

Now, though, it was time to go home.

We pushed through to the Dorman's perimeter. The sounds of something terrible trailed us.

"Just keep going!" LightBlue cried.

So we did, following the curving edges that I tried to pull from my memory.

It was close and the screams were closer.

Then, just as we were nearing the periphery, and I could feel the push that had originally caused me to explore and Rama to run, my memory becomes unreliable.

Returned: Breakfast at Tiffany's

"Sir? Sir, are you okay?" A flash of light in my eyes brought me back from the world of the Tetranne. "We got a call. Are you hurt? Do you need me to get an ambulance?" I checked myself and found that I was naked, next to a pond in an area I quickly placed as the park near the ACC.

"I…" My head pounded. "I'm sorry. Just a… a night." I covered my junk with my hands. Shame was overrated.

"I would have called the police, but, you know – I saw you at the club and, well, damned if you weren't spot on about a lot of things. Here." He handed me his Knight's Armour Security jacket and I wrapped myself in it.

"Sorry," I said. It smelled like a two-by-four.

"Bah, I've got tons of them." He looked vaguely familiar. "I can give you a lift to wherever you're staying if you like. I just got off my shift." He laughed. "I mean, I was chasing after you for a while. I thought you were going to get yourself killed in the water so I tried to get you over to the playground, but you weren't having that for long either."

"Sorry." I couldn't stop but feeling the time and experience slipping away from me.

"It's fine. The park's closed. I had Tony over there making sure you weren't getting into too much trouble. He was there, too."

"Huh?"

"Your set. We're both kinda into that scene. I can't really do what you do. Shy and stage fright."

"It's not that hard."

"Pfft. So says the king!" His radio beeped and he answered it. "He's finally coming down. I'll get him some coffee and pants and maybe…" He covered the mic. "Do you want breakfast? Tony's wife's a damn good cook." I nodded, reluctantly.

"How about brekky at your place, bud?"

The radio hissed. "Sure. Meet in ten."

Suffice it to say that the therapeutic value of a hearty, quiet breakfast cannot be overstated. Say what you will about the wonders of the worlds beyond ours, a crispy plate of bacon (or the meatless equivalent) can center you in ways the great sages of the past could only dream of.

As I crunched my way back to Earth, swaddled in a bathrobe clearly designed to accommodate Tony's gym-wrought build, I couldn't help but wonder imagine how differently things might have gone if the authorities had found me first. I resolved to extend the same courtesy to a traveler like myself in their moment of need, should I find one. As it happened, I did – but that's neither here nor there. Nor was she, for that matter.

So that about covers my experience in that strange world. I know it's not the most plausible thing in the world and that's fine with me. You'll probably think that it was a drug-fueled hallucination or a mental break but I'd have to disagree. I mean, it was drug-fueled, and it very nearly broke me, but you know what I mean.

Why, I can hear some of you asking.

Where the hell did Rama go?

Well, I'll tell you what I found out about that –

Nothing: The Dead Circle – What I Found There

So, James (the security guard) and his friend Tony turned out to be damn fine guys. I mean, it's hard not to appreciate it when someone effectively keeps you from accidentally killing yourself after you've returned from an unbelievable adventure in another reality. I told them about what happened and for the most part I think they believed me.

Alternatively, they thought it was a fun story. Which is just as good as reality sometimes.

Isn't it?

There are lots of questions that I still can't answer, though, and that's always suspicious.

Eventually we found someone who said they knew where to find the Dorman, only, when we went out to where it had been, we found a blackened circle with a white spot of ash in the shape of the anomaly that drew Rama and me into the Tetranne. I can't say it was a good feeling, exactly... I was hoping that we'd find the Dorman and Rama and LightBlue and MildlyRed, but the burn marks felt like a fine reason to keep looking... or to stop..

We placed a missing person report for Rama after a few days of waiting to see if she was going to suddenly reappear at the the ACC again. I feel a lot of guilt about the whole ordeal and, if I can take any good points from what happened that strange, wonderful evening, I was able to pull away from alcohol completely. In those first few days I started to dream up my Inner Sanctum.

A personal pantheon of people and personifications of my life that could be referred to and dealt with in a personal way instead of heading for the bottle or the drugs.

This is where, how, and why Arata was born.

A couple of more sets and a few more brekkies with the gang there, and I hopped back on the train to my next location.

Clarification: Timeline – Where I Was and How I Got Here

Now, I'm sure you're quite confused about the chronology of things. This is somewhat intentional, as I find it keeps the mind limber. However, I don't want you to be too lost. Allow me to offer you the kind courtesy of clarification on these events – let's talk about education first:

I was born in 2000, or 1999 depending where you were at the time, or which of my parents you happen to be asking – personally, my mother was traveling across the Pacific Ocean for reasons that I never got clarification on. It was a commercial flight and my father was, understandably, not present at the time.

That's right, I was a true millennial baby.

It doesn't matter where.

I left my home for a boarding school at age 6 or 7 (I can't really remember), and joined the ranks of the rootless military brats. There are plenty of stories worth discussing from this period, but now is not the time. Until I graduated and was admitted to the secondary school that affiliated with the final 3 years of primary I'd transferred in time to complete. The Ravencroft Academy. A place you can still visit, so long you are prepared to walk over its remains and imagine what it could have looked like before the fire in 2021.

I want to say that I don't know much about the situation, but that would be a lie. I wasn't responsible, though. I had begun my degree at Wilkson University, and by the time it happened I had not been within a hundred kilometres of my old stomping ground in years.

20XX (yes, twenty exty-ex – fill it in yourself if it means that much to you): I completed my undergraduate and was admitted into a fast-track for a PhD.

20XX: I successfully defended my dissertation and began my time as a more formal part of the Academic Community, such as it was. By the end of 20XX I will turn 27 years old. You can try to fight me on the maths here, but you would fail. We'll eventually get into the specifics of why this is the case.

20XX: I discover the existence of the ACC and begin to do my own sets.

20XX: I've completely disconnected from the mainstream society and have taken to the road to discover what secrets and excitement the world might hold.

20XX: I meet Rama, we enter the Tetranne, and we (?) return.

2030: I'm travelling again; it's been a while since I've been on the circuit and the events of Rama's disappearance have left me in a swelling depression. I meet a wonderful woman at my hometown, Richie, and we date for a few months before she, like the other women in my life, grows tired of my pessimism. We don't speak while I'm on the road, but she's in the crowd when I return to my ACC.

The Near-Present: Standing Out – She's Not Alone

"I spent so long living life the wrong way. I want to share this concept with you because I think there's something important about how life is and how life can be allowed to work. See, I haven't always been the collected, well-rounded person that I am today."

[Pause for laughter, if any]

"I was, and had been for so long, a person that lived in a precarious state of future-vision, unable to cope with the idea of enjoying the present at all. I can explain this phenomenon, at least I believe I can. Follow me through this:

"It all starts in our childhood. It all starts in those formative years when you think you're immortal and your impatience is based around the fact that time is perceived so painfully slowly. There are plenty of videos online that explain this better than I could. Basically, you've only had a little taste of time, so you feel like things move slowly as a result of not being to generalize and predict experiences out of natural ignorance.

"I think that school is what destroys our expectations of time. I'm not trying to suggest that school or education in general are wrong in doing so, only that due to how much time we spend there, we become conditioned for certain expectations. We want to be rewarded when we obey or repeat a fact or principle as initially presented, and we become fearful of self-exploration, of inquiry, because that might make us wrong. We gain reverence for authority figures that, in many cases, haven't figured out life any better than we will – indeed, that we have – and maybe that's a cycle we're all doomed to follow.

"Take this: We spend so much time listening and absorbing and eventually realizing that the only time we really have for our own experiences fall between the spaces when one subject is being closed and another is beginning. We learn to love the lacunae between obligations, the very concept of after school and weekends and vacations. Particularly vacations, though. How fair is it that many of us are eventually doomed to receive, as compensation, only two weeks of vacation for ourselves every year? And we are expected to be grateful for it. The conditioning began in primary school where we are left to believe that Summer vacation is a reward for our hard work throughout the year.

"Summer vacation – I mean, just think of how good that sounds, even now. I can tell by your faces that some of you have children, but for the purposes of this thought experiment, just imagine they get a vacation too, and everything is taken care of for everyone. It's the ideal. Say what you will about the promise of heaven, but I say the prospect of summer vacation can't compete.

"When we are young and as we grow, we are constantly given (and in some cases subjected to) pre-set times for relaxation and leisure. Yet, as the world betrays us, these periods shrink and shrink while the obligations we face continue to grow and grow. One is replaced by the other until, somehow, we accept the idea that we deserve almost no personal time to allow us to make enough money to sustain our lifestyle. Many people are so successfully guided down this academic to productive member of society conveyor belt that at the end they are prepared to work all day, every day, with the illusion that this is what life should be. Some of them even claim to enjoy it! Just think about that for a second. When was the last time you had a good nap?

"But it's the way that people are so quick to accept knowledge that frightens me the most. The fact that there are people who have never travelled outside their home cities is even worse. And behind closed doors and untaken roads, ignorance grows like black mould in the walls of the mind. And that actually gets to leave home. Specious arguments against things like gay marriage or science funding or humanitarian aid or vaccinations or… there are too many, really. All of this is the byproduct of education. Sit still, it tells us, and you will be rewarded. Deviate, and you are nothing.

No one.

Nobody.

"How many of you, out there in the crowd, can remember talking about a creative endeavour or a desire to be an artist with a teacher or parent, only to have them turn around and tell you to become engineer or find a practical skill? How many of you have friends that are wonderful in every way but regard your impulse for creativity and artistic development as somehow wrong?

"How is it that these same people return home after a long day of jockeying spreadsheets, or accomplishing grand and wonderful feats worthy of universal applause and adoration, and sit down on the couch with a beer – only to turn on the television and reap the benefits of entertainment created by the same people they chastise? That they condemn?

"There are other worlds out there. I've seen them – in

person, yes, but also in the eyes of the performance artists, playwrights, actors, musicians, and godforsakenly shitty poets that make life in the One City worthwhile. Ask anyone who's tried and they'll tell you: it takes time and blood to make a new world.

"But it also takes time and blood to make this world. I can condemn the City for being a soul-sucking abyss that'll take us long before our time all I want – because it is exactly that – but I wouldn't last a minute against a tiger. Or the cold. That's the trick, see. Once the City gets its teeth in you, it never lets go. But I can't fault those that keep the beast alive, for my life is bound up in it. So balance that spreadsheet, program that traffic light – hell, sell me bottled water if you need to! I'm thirsty, and I don't trust my tap.

"So what do we do? What can we do? All I can think of is this: live in this world, fight for the next, and be grateful to those who can't follow.

"But along the way, remember that too many of us live in the idea of reward and not the present. I had this problem once, and bet there are people here tonight who have not yet realized that they are doing this too. I can't say that it's easy to escape the conditioning – only that, if you try, you can start to realign your imagined self with the present self. And once you do this, why, you'll...

"Oh, I see that I've gone over my limit. Thank you for listening to my rant, and I hope you enjoyed some of my thoughts on our strange relationship with time.."

[Hold for applause, if any]

Of course, there is rarely any applause after rants like this. For whatever reasons that might be.

I said before that I was bored.

Sometimes I wonder if I'm also boring.

It's possible. I suppose.

The Couple: After My Set – Terror

"Excuse me." I turn around to find a woman and a man standing at my side, awkward and youthful but… Ah, yes.

"Ju–"

"Lisa." She says.

"Lisa! Yes, sorry. Of course. It's nice to see you again!" I reach over and give her a hug and a kiss on the cheek. Her friend doesn't seem to appreciate this.

"And this must be your boyfriend?" I assume.

"Husband."

"Right! Husband." I reach out and shake his reluctant hand.

"Nobody," I tell him.

"Richard." He vaguely murmurs.

"Well, it was nice seeing you again, but I think I'm

going to head back to my–" I honestly don't have a destination in mind, I just want to get out of this situation as quickly and quietly as possible.

"Nobody, do you remember that other time you were in town?" she asks, but I can't tell if she's trying to protect herself or if there is something else looming behind her question.

"Sure. It was, what, ten or eleven months ago?" Oh, fuck. It's all coming back to me.

"Right. Well, do you remember that I was on a bit of a split with my husband then? That we had a little... encounter?" Don't be pregnant. Don't be pregnant. Please, oh god, don't be pregnant.

"We had a good time, didn't we?" I'm sweating a goddamned river.

"It was... a change that I needed, yes. Only, do you remember that story you were telling when you visited last time?"

"Sort of."

Shape"It was about how you had this crazy adventure with a woman named Rama. You said that she vanished afterwards, but that it was one of the most memorable experiences that you'd ever had. There was all this amazing imagery that involved a strange allegorical world and creatures that spoke in color! I can remember like it was yesterday because it was like you were speaking directly to me and how I felt about life. It made me feel completely different. I thought we were torn from the same cloth and so when we started to speak afterwards... well, you wouldn't drink but we had a few hits off that bong in the back and then we made our way back to my place. Do you remember how you offhandedly mentioned that after you came back from there, in the midst of that spiral of depression and self-loathing, that you just kind of made up a guy in your head? You didn't seem to have very many – just one. You never named him when you brought him up, but..." Arata.

"Yes? What about him?"

The little man in an almost comically tiny beanie spoke up at last.

"Did he look like this?" He held up a sketch.

Shinji Arata: The Doctor – The Disease

"I... Uh..." It's him. It's 100% him! How the capital-F Fuck did... "How the fuck... What is this? What are you... Whaaaa?" I can be quite eloquent sometimes.

"I'll take that as a yes," she said.

"I don't think I quite get what's going on here."

"Richard is the one who came up with the theory, so I'll let him tell you." She turned to her short husband who stretched himself a little taller as he cleared his throat and started in what would, I was sure, count among the strangest things I'd ever heard.

"You and Lisa slept together, right?" He held up his hand to save me from additional stammering. "It's fine. We've had this chat. I needed to know because only if that's true does

any of this make any sense. And that's stretching the term.
See, I figure, somehow you must have picked something off of
that Rama woman. She was Japanese, right? Maybe there's…
I just call it a neurovirus.

I'm sure there's a better term or way to explain it.
Whatever. So, you got it from that woman and then you gave
it to Lisa. We got back together about three months ago and,
well, after we got back together, well, I started to have these…
flashes. Or visions. Or, uh, I don't want to sound like a broken
record but… whatever the hell it is. Sometimes they were just
abstract feelings and sometimes it was like I was where he
was. I could taste his food. I could see him going about his
business and then, poof. Back to normal."

"Neurovirus?" I considered this, playing the
implications out in my mind. "Are you saying… it's like a…
mental… neurological…

STD?"

"I guess that's a way to put it." He sighed.

I looked at them. Paused. Waited for something to
follow like: Haha, just kidding. But nothing followed. Just
absent, albeit concerned, stares.

"So. So… Sooo? What do, what do… Uh."
Eloquence.

"It gets weirder." Oh great. "After we compared our
experiences we started to do some searching. You know, just a
light digging here and there. And we found this–" Lisa handed
me a few sheets of printed paper.

I read it: Arata, Shinji. Ichinomiya, Aichi Prefecture, Japan.

"No. Fucking. Way."

"Haha – look, he said the same thing you did!" Lisa laughed as Richard scowled.

"Look. Nobody. We're going to Japan. We've got tickets. We're heading off tonight." I was at a loss for words but, thankfully, found enough of them to respond.

"Good luck with that madness." I was ready to get away when Richard held out a ticket in my direction.

"We're all going." He glared. "You started this. Don't you want to get to the bottom of it?"

"Do I want to go meet a guy that I thought was a figment of my imagination until all of five minutes ago, but who is somehow intimately related to my… intimacy? Do I want to find out what the hell is going on with my life up to this point, even though the whole damned world might explode when we get too close to the universal law?" I paused. Took the ticket. "Yes, I do. Sounds like fun."

Airborne: Character Profiles – Star-crossed Lovers

We left North America and expected to arrive at Narita International Airport the following day. It's one of those things that you appreciate more when you're traveling back in the opposite direction. Still, the lost time was enough for the three of us to chat a lot about... life and all those fun bits.

It didn't take long to figure out why Lisa and I were so compatible when we met. Despite his stature (which we can't really fault him on), Richard and I shared a remarkable number of similarities. He, like me, had had a difficult time adjusting to the demands of normalcy. He had broken free of that when he founded a dotcom web service back in the 90s. It was a story of untold millions and crushing bankruptcy.

A modern tragic figure, he was. Now, he supported the two of them through consultation services that took him away from home pretty often. Lisa somewhat understandably wanted a family and couldn't let that happen until Richard settled down in a single place. They argued, words were said, and a relationship of ten years faltered... and was revitalized, somewhat painfully, by her mistake with me.

All things considered, he was awfully composed about the situation we found ourselves in.

Ex-lover, and all that.

Supernaturally infectious ex-lover, I mean.

Lisa, well, she was an artist, wasn't she?

Loved to paint and had some really neat-o things, too. But she only sold maybe one or two a year, and that wasn't nearly enough to support their future on. So, reluctantly, she went back to work in a huge office doing graphic design for smaller offices and companies. It paid the bills. Some might say it was worth it. But all that stress had been the catalyst for their problems. Now, though, they were united by the strangeness that I had brought into their lives.

Call me fucking Cupid.

We watched a film.

We slept for a few hours.

And we awoke as the Red Sun rose in and burned at the backside of our metal carriage. Through customs, onto a bus, into a queue for train tickets and then off-off-and-away on the bullet train we went towards the innocuous city of Ichinomiya to meet our collective fates and/or destroy reality when we came face to face with our psychologically-bound salaryman.

Nihon: Lonely City – Lost Promises

The train rolls up to a city that, Wikipedia tells me, has a population in the range of 350,000 people.

It has an official flower (how cute): The Chinese Bellflower.

As well as a tree: The Round-Leaf Holly.

Ichinomiya apparently means The First Shrine. Which seemed somehow appropriate given that we were all on a pilgrimage of sorts.

That's about all the time I had to research before we found ourselves carried away by the scenery that went from Tokyo to Nagoya. Here, we switched trains and found ourselves chugging by at far less breakneck speeds, cutting away from the towers of the metropolis and out to the distant countryside. We sliced through mountains, crept above rushing rivers, and eventually, well, we were there.

Stepping out of the station, we caught a taxi, with a clean and well-groomed driver complete with white gloves and iconic black hat. The doors swung open at a push of a button and with a quick Google translation, we were off to the Aoiyume office just a few blocks away.

The buildings there were a mixed batch of clean, crisp and deliberate structures, some freshly tiled and others whose gray-beige tones hinted at the vibrant colours of a more prosperous past. It was the telltale sign of either a city in the early stages of decay, or one reluctant to change to meet the modern era. Perhaps it couldn't decide.

"We're here." Richard tapped on the glass separating the passengers and our driver, and he pulled over. Money was exchanged, doors swung open again and...

"This isn't what I was expecting." We were all struck dumb by the scene, tired by our flight and exhausted by the trains. This was a sign we weren't prepared to deal with.

We looked back to the driver, who shrugged. "Kurosudo," he said.

"Huh?" Richard thought for a moment. "Uh."

"Hoteru?" the driver asked, clearly familiar with this conversation.

"No thanks," Richard said, eager to get moving. "Okay. We're going to look around." The driver didn't catch this at first, and waved before heading off to pick up his next fare.

We weren't deterred for too long, though. At least, not Lisa, who had already walked straight up to the door and started giving it a good hammering like it would miraculously op— It opened.

"I'll be damned," Richard and I said in perfect unison.

"Well?" Lisa headed inside before we could say anything to stop her. Naturally, we followed. Inside, the building seemed to be frozen in time. At the flick of a switch, lights twinkled into existence across a panorama of dozens of cubicles, surrounded by a ring of offices.

"This. This is the place!" It took a second for me to recognize my own voice. I don't usually get excited, but...

"Come on!" Lisa rushed forward across the immaculate office building, without even so much as a wastebasket to stop her. I was clear that someone had been keeping this place clean. Crossing through intersections distinguished from one another by larger (and shinier) name placards on desks, we found our way to the only office that we could collectively remember.

Then we stopped.

"You do it." Lisa turned to me.

Fine, I thought. I wanted answers as much as the others, if not more so. I reached for the door and there was a click behind me.

"Gaijin-da?" The woman was small and old.

"Hello." Richard waves. "Do you know Shin-ji A-ra-ta?"

"Idiots," the woman said, shaking her head. "I speak English. What are you doing here?"

"The door was open." Lisa countered, a little too quickly to project any modicum of innocence.

"And how were we supposed to know you speak English?" Lisa added. "I'm sorry to have offended you. We've traveled a long way to speak with someone here."

She considered this for a moment, placing her duster to the side and stretching a bit. She smiled, suddenly appearing to have understood what had to be going on.

"You must be the investors. I'm sorry, but we are closed today. Can you come back tomorrow? We will have tea and you can speak with the President." She pointed us towards the door. "I can arrange for hotel rooms and an executive car for your visit." She bowed as she moved us away from our destination and out to the street.

We were too stunned by her courtesy and apparent rank to do anything but listen and obey.

She flipped open her phone and in minutes a fancy, black leather-upholstered car pulled up next to us with a foreign driver at the helm.

"If you need anything, please call me." She handed us a business card. Entering the cab, our driver smiled and welcomed us.

"Yuriko-San can be a little intense, eh? She's a doll, though. Really likes to make sure everyone is happy and in good form.

The name's Pete. How can I be of assistance, folks?"

Ichinomiya: The Centre of the World – Ins, Outs, and Abouts

"You sure you won't have one?" Richard looked at me with his inquisitive eyes.

"Haven't had a drink in a while. Won't start now."

"Leave him be, dear." Lisa sipped her beer and adjusted herself on the tall stool as Pete ordered us food.

It didn't take too long before I started to feel the crush of jet, train, and shared-dream lag, and I decided to head back to the room before my... uh, Inner Arata took hold and convinced me to get shitfaced with the lovely couple and the Canadian cabbie. I didn't have the energy to spite him with sobriety.

The streets were picturesque in their cleanliness. The trees, green and lush. The people smiled and spoke in quick, untranslatable bursts that quieted on my approach and rose again as the distance grew.

I wasn't far from where we checked in, the Shin-Ichinomiya Ryokan, a fancy, traditional-style hotel (at least I assumed it was; I'm no expert)) – when I felt a hand on my shoulder.

"Come with me," an oddly familiar voice said. "You and your friends are in great danger."

Desperate: The Outside Arata – Almost Answers

We walked down into a small izakaya, a bar-restaurant, at the end of a street where the lights were so dim I could barely make out my own hands. The candles on tables seemed like stars strewn across a great abyss, with our eyes barely reflecting the light in the distance. It's the kind of place you go when you want to be unseen and unnoticed. I broke the silence. "How did you find me?" The man ordered us some drinks.

"Arata?" Of course I recognized him. But here all I could think of is the fact that the world didn't come to an end when he grabbed me earlier. I confess to having been a little disappointed. I rather wanted to see that happen again.

"And You. The man who likes to be called Nobody." He lit a smoke and offered me one. I took it and we sat while smoke filled our lungs in a vacuum-thick silence. The drinks arrived and he raised his to me. "To our glory days. May they last forever!" he stammered. He was already drunk, which didn't really jibe with my understanding of what Meeting One's Destiny was supposed to involve, but suited what I knew of Arata just fine. I sniffed the alcohol, not that I had any intention of drinking it.

"It's sweat potato."

"Sweet," I corrected him. He shrugged.

"Why have you come here?" A ring of smoke left his mouth and hovered above his glass like a halo.

"I – we have questions. Why the hell do we keep seeing you in our heads?"

This didn't surprise him as much as I thought it would.

"A bleed… We should have caught this earlier…" he said to himself and then faced me. "You can't be here. It is very dangerous for you to be here."

"Why?"

"Because. Your accounts have been…" He considered. "Discontinued."

"Meaning?"

"I will explain everything. But not here. I need you to go get your friends and make it look casual. Then, I want you to take a taxi – not that corporate dog car – a real taxi and get them to drive you to my friend's house at the lake about an hour north of here."

I nodded. "I've seen it."

Again, this didn't seem to concern him.

"Good. Meet me there and I will tell you everything. You can't tell anyone that you've seen me, though. This is of the utmost importance." He finished his drink and slipped away into the darkness.

Diversion: Leaves of Pink – Opportunities for an Ending

I retraced my steps to the other bar and found the others in a state of alcoholic decay (or preservation; poisoning and pickling are two sides of same bottle). The driver, though, he looked at me with those inquisitive eyes that I've come to know so well from my time at the ACC.

"Come back, have ya?"

"Couldn't sleep."

"Oh, you leave him be, Petey!" Lisa had the drunk-eye. You know, that one that happens when your mind decides you don't qualify for depth perception anymore and you are forced to stagger your way through the world, often resulting in bruising and... occasional exits from our home dimension?

"It's fine. I just wanted to see if I could come back and convince you to both to get some sleep before our big meeting tomorrow." I shrugged. "Lots to discuss. Wouldn't want you to... be too messed up." I looked at Richard, who was more sober but still on the

I'mma smile at you for no reason stage of the drunken personality spectrum.

"Jus...Jusss... Yeah. Okay. I could sleep," he realized. "Are you sure? I can bring you to some fun clubs if you want." Pete's emphasis on fun went over everyone's head but mine. "They're open all night."

"I'm good," I tell him. "Let's get the lady to bed, shall we?" I nudged Richard and he scowled.

"Fine, ffffine, Mister ushy here wants to sleep so we should all sleep. Isn't enough that you have to go around fooling about with people's wives and god-knows-what-else, but you gotta control the whole-wide-world, don'tcha?!"

He stood up and stared me in the chest, prodding it with his tiny finger.

"I said... don'tcha?!"

If I had wanted to be a babysitter, I would have said so. I decided to let Richard feel as right as he wanted to be. "Yes, sure, whatever it takes to help you get some sleep. We have important things to discuss so we might as well be sober for it, no?"

Having completely missed what I said, Lisa began to play the peacemaker. "Rich, come on, let's just..." She suddenly looked a little green. "Oh... OH, god. I..." She gagged. "Get. Me. To. Bed," she commanded, and her husband quickly latched on and got her vertical.

"What do we owe on the bill?" I asked.

Peter waved his hand. "The company will cover it. You guys get some rest, I'll settle here. Can you make it back without me?" I nod and we all left.

Taxi Ride: Away – Arata by the Lake

"So. He's real." Richard shook his head. "I mean. He's really real, like, for real."

"He is," I told him.

"So, we're off to see the wizard, are we?" Lisa was

sobering up, but wasn't quite there yet. The taxi had been out the light pollution of Ichinomiya for a good hour, and the driver had taken us off of paved roads, so we couldn't have been far.

"What else did he tell you?" Richard asked.

"Nothing else. Just what I said."

"Fuuuck... would you look at that!" A small lantern flickered outside a small but beautiful temple standing at the edge of a calm lake. Or pond, as I'd prefer it be called. If you can swim across it, it's not really that much of a lake. We paid the taxi and we approach the front door. Arata was waiting for us.

"He's fucking real!" Richard rushed up and started to survey the man, gesticulating wildly as he shook off the last vestiges of disbelief.

"Look! Lisa! He's real – just like I imagined him!"

"We imagined him."

"I'm real," Arata said, smiling at the compliment. "Certainly good to know. Please," he said as he ushered us forward, "Come in." We took off our shoes and the door closed behind us.

"I am sure you have many questions, but I believe I can best explain what you are by describing where we are. This temple and the lands beyond belonged to my family for generations and generations. But there was a division between brothers, sometime after the Second World War. So many had lost their faith in the nation and the land, and it was abandoned. But death has a way of settling the bitterest feuds. My father returned after discovering the deed, and spent years thereafter restoring it." He pointed to the far wall. "Bombs had almost entirely buried the rear of the temple under the mud of Lake Ichie. But, over patient decades, he was able to raise it. I never found out how. Some things remain as mysterious to us as they seemed in our youth. Some things we never understand. Perhaps that is as it should be." He smiled and offered us a seat by a small fireplace in the centre of a tatami room. Everyone remained standing.

"When my brothers and I started to come here, he forbade us from swimming. Apparently people were known to go missing out on the murky, lifeless waters. Still, my father bought a boat and he enjoyed going out to the middle to relax and paint. This is one of his." He pointed at a beautiful scene of the temple from the water hanging from the branches of a tree just to the side of the room. It had grown so large that its trunk extended into the neighbouring chamber.

"He said he felt a great pull in the lake. It was, for him, a creative muse. And for whatever reason, when he found this sapling sprouting into the temple, he encouraged it to take a place of honour. As if it were a manifestation of ancient spirits. He said it was a celebration of life, and it grew majestically after the war. My father loved it, possibly more than the temple itself, and often spoke to it as though it knew what he was saying. For him, it was a sign of the resilience of nature and the determination of his spirit." He laughed. "Now, though, it has grown too large and I have had to trim branches to keep the roof from collapsing. Like grasping arms desperate to escape."

Although I had tried to hide it, Arata saw my anxiety. "I know this place is safe because none survive today save for me that appreciate its existence and understand its connection to my family. The war destroyed the historical records. And my father destroyed the deed, long ago." He turned back to the tree. "This tree, healthy but obstructive, is the last real link I have to him. When I amputated these limbs years ago, when my father was still alive, he grew distant and furious. Upon discovering what I had done, he promised that he would never endow it to me. This is why I know this place is safe."

He scanned our expressions and then, with a curious shimmer in his eyes, looked at me.

"Nobody owns it."

He burst out laughing, but neither our time inside Arata's head, nor his in ours, gave us no insight as to why.

He checked his pockets. "I don't suppose any of you have a smoke?"

I shook my head, as did Lisa. Then, somewhat bashfully, Richard presented some.

"Richard!" Lisa shouted. "When did you take up smoking again?"

"This isn't the time for that, is it?" He passed them over.

"Thank you. Now, as I was saying, there are some things in life that we must accept because we may never learn their secrets." He tossed some wood onto the fire. "But! For you, at least one of those mysteries will be revealed. You want to know what connects us all? You want to know what has been going on at Aoiyume and why it has reached you – and this, I can tell you." We looked on, incredulously. This was going to be good.

"My name is Shinji Arata. This you know. I am fifty-four years old and I have been living in Japan my entire life. I learned English from an Eikaiwa and then studied Social Engineering at Tokyo University. I met a man there. The only foreigner I can remember being admitted to our program. He was tall and friendly, in a way. We became good friends. We spoke about everything. Philosophy. Love. Hate. War and peace. We went out drinking and one day we came upon a small izakaya outside of Shinjuku. Here, everything changed. We were welcomed to a place that not only allowed but actually encouraged free-thinking and abstract thought. It rewarded the artist and the scientist alike. We spoke about the past and the future and the War."

He pulled a cigarette from his pocket, the symbol of the Violent Belle printed on the filter, and carefully lit it amongst embers that had escaped the fireplace.

"I can say that we were best friends and that, even today, I can count him as the person that understands me the most."

I stood, my patience running thin. "What does this even remotely have to do with–" Arata's finger went up.

"We were invited to a gathering in Nara. A city that was once the centre of Japanese culture and politics, where everything was forced to change." He let out circles of smoke. "I was hesitant, but my friend was instantly convinced."

"He accepted the offer and since that time, over twenty-years have gone by since our last encounter." He grew quiet.

"So sad." Lisa nudged past Richard and gave Arata a pat on the back. "What happened to your friend?" I asked.

Lisa's sympathy evaporated. "Who cares? Tell us what's happening to us already!"

He sighed. "I'm almost there. This, I believe, is important. So: I tried to stay in contact with him, but the position he took sent him out, across the world. While I, after some hesitation and discussion with my wife, accepted a similar offer. I can't really get into details about what happened from there to now, there's simply too much. What you'll care to know is that I defected a month ago. The company does not like defectors. So, I took some of my hardcopies as a form of insurance that they would leave me alone. Most of it will mean nothing to you to, but some..." He stood up. "Please, this way."

We followed him through the monks' sleeping quarters and a few other rooms I could not identify to the back of the temple where a smaller tatami room with a bedroll was neatly stacked in the corner next to a few boxes.

"These will begin to help you understand." He opened the first and handed me a stack of paper, written in English with Japanese, I assume, translating the details. No!

I glanced around and picked out pieces as they appeared across dozens of pages, realizing what they were as I relived the past.

This, in no particular order, is what they looked like:

My Inner Reality: The Apothecary – Arata

Looking Back: Who I was – and What I Wasn't

Sidestory: The English Door – Pimm's Definition

"What am I looking at here?" I asked him. "What the FUCK am I looking at?"

"May I ask you a question, Nobody?" I nodded. Why

not?

"When I spoke of the club that I was part of in University, did it not strike you as… familiar?" He turned to the others. "How about you?"

I had an inkling, but and Lisa and Richard were still hung over.

"It does, doesn't it?"

"Are you saying that they are connected?" I asked.

"They are."

Being so close to an answer had never made me this angry before. "How?"

"To find people. To discover those among us that are incapable of living in the world as it is and want to believe in the promise of something better. Something more..." He put out one cigarette and started another. "They are, for lack of a better term, training camps. They are used to cultivate agents with the capacity to bring about great change and either put them to work creating their world, or remove them from circulation."

"Then what?"

He was smiling. "That depends on whether they like what they see."

"It's too much." Richard rubbed his face in his hands. "It's too fucking much."

"I know what you're capable of, Nobody. They would have come for you eventually. But after the bleed, well, that must have put you on their radar early, must have made them nervous. Our... systems were breached. Somehow." Arata picked up a sheet he had taken from the pile earlier. "I think it was this. I think it was the place you visited. The Tetranne. We've never encountered someone who has returned through one of the Dolmen Gates."

Dolmen? I thought. I must have mispronounced it to LightBlue.

Arata handed the sheet to me.

It was different from the first. Analysed. Collected. Informative.

I looked at who signed the order.

"Is this right?" He nodded.

"Precedent. Not President?"

He nodded again. "As in those who set the precedents. They are the guiding forces for change, and for social and political progress.

They created the ACC, and the ACC creates their new world."

"But... Pimm?"

"Pimm?" Lisa spat as she spoke.

"You mean President Pimm?" Richard added. "That crazy owner of the club back home?"

"Apparently… uh… not so crazy?"

"I can't tell you much more than that, really. It gets darker and goes deeper than you can even fathom." Arata coughed. "But now that you know…" He coughed again. "Now that you know…" Blood dripped from his mouth. "Ah. I see." He sat down.

"What's wrong?"

"They know what we I done – what we have done." Arata struggled to say. "They will be here soon." He looked at us. "One of you has betrayed us…"

"They? Who the hell are they? And what do you mean by us?!" Lisa frantically searched the room for clues. "Who would betray us? We've been together the whole –" She stopped, turned around, and knew.

"All this time?" she asked Richard.

"Not all of it. Pimm asked me to keep tabs on you after he discovered that you and this guy had a little fling. I didn't really think we would get back together, butr…" He began to walking away, heading towards the nearest exit, but I cut him off.

"Why would you do it? What could he possible give you?!" she screamed.

"I wish I could tell you, Lis. I wish you could see the

world as he has made me see it. I'm so much more than I was when we left each other. I… know more than I ever believed was possible." He waved his hands in the air. "It's all a facade! It's all an illusion… Gods be good, if you even knew a fraction of what was going on… if you even knew what… what's going to happen to humanity, well, fuck, you'd beg me to kill you. No one who hasn't passed the Trials should be allowed into that future. No one."

He ran past me, pushing me aside with more strength than I could have imagined coming from such a small man. Our resident turncoat was just full of surprises. .

"Don't!" I grabbed Lisa as she rushed after him.

"We have to get him! He's–"

Lights exploded like grenades from the shoreline at the front of the temple, through the sheets of paper walls, through the opening where the moonlight had illuminated us.

It was everywhere – like the counterfeit daylight of a false star.

Footsteps, hurried and heavy, echoed from the other side.

"They're here!" Arata's words escaped with spurts of blood.

"What… What do we do?"

"Help me up. I know a way." So we did and brought him to the water.

Warnings from a Light in the Sky – The Lie and the Promise

"A boat? I don't think that will help us much," Lisa said, but he insisted – and in the absence of any other options, we obeyed. The engine sputtered to life and launched forward just as we removed the rope from the dock.

Arata was fading, his face a cool shade of pearl, and yet, he seemed aware enough of us and where we were so we listened to him.

Nearly halfway across, he demanded we stop.

"Down," he said.

Lisa didn't say anything but I could read it on her face.

She felt it too.

"Is it… another Dolmen?" But Arata was silent, his breathing slow.

He had no time left.

We took each other in hand and lept off into the cold, dark water, following the pull into a swirling vortex, and just as I felt my lungs heave their last gasp of air and my eyes catch their last

glimpse of light…

Where We Go/Went: Eyes Open – See a New World

* * *

Some Time Later

I closed the binder. "That was the last time I saw them. Something happened in that lake, Precedent Pimm. To speak of what it was, I cannot say, and if you asked me to speculate I would be at a loss for words. If you hadn't arrived we might have..." I stop just short of blaming them for ruining my cover. Everything else I've told them is the truth, but it probably won't matter. I will likely be punished as a reminder to the others of the price we pay for our knowledge, power, and privileges.

I wait in silence.

No one says anything, although the look on their faces speaks of unanimous disappointment that we lost track of an unclaimed Lie and another Dolmen.

Three Inevitable Truths. Eight Shadowed Lies.

And Beyond Them All –

█████████

That's what they always told us, right?

Now I wonder. What does that really mean? What is

this OoNnEe and why have we been chasing after it for so long? We found a Lie a long time ago, and It (or She – or He) changed the way we looked at the world. Seeing behind the veil, even for a moment, gave us power.

But who can you trust when you work behind the scenes… but struggle to escape an absurdist play of your own? I wait in the dimly lit chamber, glaring eyes and grimaces my only company, until, without a word, the Heralds leave. Finally, even Precedent Pimm is gone.

I'm alone and left to my thoughts.

Part of me hopes that, wherever my friends went – and however I betrayed them, they were definitely my friends – that they found a world beyond the shadows that drown our own.

B C WOODRUFF

Montréal-born Brian Woodruff is a writer
and bibliophile with an appreciation for life,
the universe and nearly everything.

IAN MORGENHEIM

A lifelong love of gaming and a stroke of
baffling luck led writer/editor Ian
Morgenheim a third of the way across the
world. Things have only gotten better.

www.ingramcontent.com/pod-product-compliance
Lightning Source LLC
Chambersburg PA
CBHW020612180626
46810CB00007B/2745